SHOOT-OUT

Shem hesitated, his gun drawn, darting a glance toward the beautiful girl with the Dance revolver. Tearing ever closer came a blond giant afork a huge blood bay stallion. . . .

Tossing his left leg across the saddlehorn, Mark Counter dropped to the ground while his big horse still ran at speed. Shem swung toward him, revolver slanting in his direction. Down swooped Counter's right hand in an effortless lightning move. All in one incredibly swift action, the right side Army Colt flowed from its holster, cocked, and fired. Its bullet caught Shem in the chest . . . Shem crashed to the ground, but he felt nothing, for the blond giant's bullet had burst through his heart.

"Howdy, Belle," the blond said in greeting as he moved forward cautiously to make sure Shem no longer posed any problem. "Looks like you're in trouble, as usual."

Also by J. T. Edson

THE NIGHTHAWK
NO FINGER ON THE TRIGGER

THE
BAD BUNCH

J. T. Edson

A DELL BOOK

Published by
Dell Publishing
a division of
Bantam Doubleday Dell
Publishing Group, Inc.
666 Fifth Avenue
New York, New York 10103

ISBN: 0-440-20764-9

Printed in the United States of America

Published simultaneously in Canada

October 1990

10 9 8 7 6 5 4 3 2 1

OPM

*For W.O. II "Bill" Day, R.A.V.C. rtd.,
all is forgiven.*

1

THE RAVAGED VILLAGE

The last time they saw the small village it had been a peaceful haven on the banks of the Ouachita River's Oak Creek, passed over by the tide of war, which swept across much of Arkansas. From all appearances, the peace had ended in no uncertain manner. Although fires no longer burned and the previous night's rains had even wiped away the smoke, blackened timbers rose stark and grim among the wreckage of the houses. Bodies lay scattered around. Men, women, and children sprawled in death; made more hideous, if possible, by the clear blue sky and warm sun of a glorious late May's day.

Halting their horses on top of a rim overlooking the village, the two riders stared down in disbelief, then horror, although neither was exactly unused to violent death. Captain Dustine Edward Marsden Fog bit down an exclamation as he studied the scene. At his side, the lean, Indian-dark sergeant gave a low grunt.

"We're on the right trail, Cap'n Dusty," he said.

"It looks that way, Kiowa," agreed the man rated by many as one of the Confederate States' army's three top

fighting commanders and the best on the Arkansas bat-
tlefront.

At first glance Dusty Fog did not appear to fit in with
his reputation. His height would not exceed five foot six
inches, although his shoulders had a width that hinted
at considerable strength. Dusty blond hair showed from
under the brim of his white Jeff Davis campaign hat and
its brim threw a shadow on a tanned, strong, good-
looking face. Though the face had strength, it looked
even younger than its eighteen years when in repose.
At that moment, gray eyes slitted and lips drawn tight,
it showed something of the man tempered by war and
command over others. His tunic had been well tailored,
but bore signs of much use. Double breasted in the
formal manner, it ended at waist level, without the
skirt's "extending halfway between hip and knee" as
required by dress regulations. Like the tunic, his
breeches had seen long service, but his boots showed
they had been kept in good repair. Around his waist
hung a western-style gun belt, matched ivory-handled
1860 Army Colts riding butt forward in the contoured
fast-draw holsters. He rode a big black stallion astride a
low-horned, double-girthed range saddle. Under his left
leg lay a Spencer carbine in a saddle boot, while a
Haiman Brothers saber rode on the right side, secured
to the horn.

The man at Dusty's side had a face that told of Indian
blood, and wore a worn uniform with three chevrons on
the sleeves. Like his officer, he possessed good leather-
work and carried well-cared-for arms.

While Dusty and Kiowa sat staring at the ravaged
village, the remainder of Company C approached under the command of First Lieutenant Red Blaze. Any
student of cavalry tactics as practiced by Dusty Fog
would have deduced that the company did not ride on
an ordinary mission. Normally those hard-bitten veterans relied upon their Colts, such rifles as they might

possess, and sabers when in action. In addition to their normal weapons, they had along a sharpshooter armed with a heavy, powerful rifle that bore a barrel-long telescopic sight, while at the rear of the column came four mules carrying a dismantled mountain howitzer and its ammunition.

At that time, with the fortunes of the war more and more favoring the Union, the Texas Light Cavalry were probably the best-equipped, -armed and -mounted regiment in the Confederate army. Commanded by leaders skilled in horseback fighting, they followed the Napoleonic tradition of making war support war. Although backed by rich Texans and with the resources of the Lone Star State at their disposal, they also relied on raiding their Yankee opponents to supply their more specialized needs. Always outnumbered, Ole Devil Hardin held Arkansas for the Confederacy and forced the Yankees to expend much effort that might have been used on other battlefronts. Had the Southern states been able to supply him with more men, arms, and equipment, he might have made an even greater contribution, even turned the course of the war.

Dusty thought of none of that as he looked down on the village. All he knew was that his present mission suddenly assumed a grim and deadly importance.

"We'll move down, ready for trouble," he told Kiowa. "Likely they'll've gone, but we'll not chance it."

"Sure," grunted the sergeant.

Ideally a company consisted of eighty men, five sergeants, four corporals, a farrier, two wagoners, two musicians, and a saddler. Action's casualties, illness, and other causes reduced Dusty's company to fifty men, not counting the sharpshooter and five artillery men who served and handled the howitzer. Not too large a force for the assignment on hand. Nor had Dusty ever been one for recklessly risking the lives of the men under his command.

Galloping ahead of the company, Red Blaze joined his cousin on the rim. Tall, tanned, and freckled, Red was Dusty's age and wore a similar uniform, though with the badges of a first lieutenant as against his cousin's triple-bar captain's insignia. Normally Red's face held a look of pugnacious cheer and good spirits, but not as he looked down on the village.

"Goddamn it, Dusty—" he burst out.

"First three fours with me as skirmishers, Red," Dusty interrupted. "Hold the rest to cover us."

"Yo!" Red answered, giving the accepted cavalry assent to an order.

On command, the leading twelve men joined Dusty and fanned out into a single line. With their guns drawn, they prepared to ride down the slope.

"Cap'n Dusty!" called a voice.

Turning in his saddle, Dusty looked to where a soldier broke ranks in the main body and rode toward him. About to snap a command sending the man back to position, Dusty stopped, the words unsaid. One glance at the soldier's face told Dusty that something of importance caused the breach of discipline. Like any good commander, Dusty knew every man under him. Tracey Prince had served in Company C for over a year, in that time gaining a reputation for courage and possessing a roving eye for the ladies. Only something of exceptional importance would have brought such concern to Prince's face.

"What is it?" Dusty asked before the sergeant major could blare out an order to Prince.

"I'd like the cap'n's permission to go down there, right now."

"Why?"

"I know some folks down in the village."

Which most likely meant Prince knew a girl. During the time Dusty rode accompanied by a small force on a mission that saved Texas from the ravages of an Indian war,* Red took the company on a raiding patrol and spent three days camped by the village until the horses recovered from the exertions put upon them. Belonging to the Quaker faith, the people of the village took no sides in the war and made Confederate or Union men equally welcome. Probably Prince met a girl who attracted his attention and wanted to learn of her fate.

"Come with us," Dusty said. "Only remember that we're going there as skirmishers, not to look for friends."

Watched by Red and the remainder of the company, Dusty's party advanced on the village. Born and reared on the Texas range country, they kept to their horses instead of dismounting to go in on foot. If a fight came, the Texas Light Cavalry preferred to do it Indian fashion and from the back of a horse.

Alert and ready for trouble, the skirmishers entered the village. Low curses came at the sights that met their eyes, hardened veterans though every one of them might be. There had been murder, looting, torture, rape, and mutilation. It seemed that those who died fighting—what fighting such peaceable folks could do—had been the lucky ones.

Passing through the village, Dusty's party saw no living person. On reaching the opposite side to which he entered, the young captain halted his men.

"It's like the Comanche jumped them!" breathed one man. "Not one left alive."

"That's allus been Hannah's way," a second went on.

With an effort Dusty regained control of himself. Fury and revulsion had filled him at what he saw, but he knew he must hold himself in check and take no chances. They might be on the edge of the fighting area, yet that did not preclude the chance of meeting the enemy.

* Told in *The Devil Gun*.

"Take the men to the high ground there, Kiowa," he said. "Corporal Gray, put out pickets. You see if you can find any sign, Kiowa."

"Yo!" replied the two men.

"Go look for your friends, Tracey," Dusty went on, seeing the anguish on the soldier's face.

Only discipline had held Prince in the line so long. Given permission, he turned his horse and galloped back to a burned-out house. Dusty followed, watching the soldier leap down and charge through what had been the building's front door. Dismounting, Dusty followed Prince inside. A charred body lay under a fallen beam, and another at the fireplace. Dusty thrust past the soldier and forced himself to make an examination of the bodies.

"A man," he said, indicating the shape under the beam. "The other was a woman. . . . Easy there, Tracey, I'd say it's not the one you're looking for."

"I-It's not Rowena," Prince confirmed in a strangled voice as he looked at what had been a plump figure. "Oh God! She's not in here."

Dusty's attention went to the fireplace and he stepped forward to look at a part of the flooring that had been raised to expose a small cavity. Such a spot was often used as a hiding place for money and other valuables, although the one into which he peered held nothing.

"Let's go, Tracey," Dusty said quietly.

"I've got to find her!" Prince shouted, staring wildly around him. "Maybe there's a cellar—"

With that he flung himself toward some more charred wood that had formed part of the roof. Dusty saw that the soldier might easily collapse the entire building on them and stepped forward.

"Easy, Tracey!" he snapped, gently gripping the other's arm.

"Go to hell!" Prince began, trying to free himself.

Swinging the soldier around to face him, Dusty struck as taught him by his uncle, Ole Devil Hardin's personal servant. Many people thought Tommy Okasi to be Chinese, although he claimed to hail from Japan. No matter where he came from, the little Oriental knew some mighty fancy fighting tricks and passed them on to Dusty.

So when the small Texan struck Prince in the stomach, he did not use his clenched fist. Instead he kept his fingers extended and together, the thumb bent over the upturned palm, and thrust them hard into Prince's solar plexus. Just how effective the *hira-nukite*, level-piercing hand blow of karate, was showed in the way Prince croaked and doubled over. Still keeping the hand in the same manner, Dusty struck again. This time he used the *shuto*, hand sword, driving the base of his hand around to strike the nape of Prince's neck. Down went the soldier, collapsing like a back-broken rabbit.

"Sorry, Tracey," Dusty said, and bent down to take hold of the other under the armpits.

By the time Dusty had drawn the unconscious soldier out of the house, he found Red bringing the rest of the company toward the building. Not all of them, though. Red might be a hotheaded young cuss with a penchant for becoming involved in fights, but he acted cool enough in his duties. Before following his cousin, Red left four men to watch their rear.

"What happened to Tracey?" Red asked, joining Dusty.

"He was looking for a gal he knew. Tell the men to leave the horses outside the village, Red. Off-saddle, feed, and water. Then we'll need a burial detail."

"Yo!" Red replied. "I'll send somebody to tend to him."

"Be best. Tell Billy Jack to join me."

Accompanied by his tall, gangling, mournful-looking, but very efficient sergeant major, Dusty made another round of the town. The small Texan forced himself to examine bodies and looked into buildings, but he saw nobody who might have so attracted Prince's attention.

"Maybe Hannah's bunch took her off alive with 'em," the sergeant major said.

"Maybe," Dusty replied. "I hope she's dead."

"Lively and right pretty li'l gal, by all accounts," Billy Jack continued.

"How'd you mean?"

"Hear tell she acted a mite too free for a Quaker person's daughter. Might be that she just got all excited at seeing some new young faces around."

Dusty looked at the sergeant major and read nothing in the miserable features. Yet Billy Jack never wasted words on idle gossip and must have some reason for making the statement. An interruption came before Dusty could ask questions.

Two riders galloped over the rim, by the pickets left by Red and down in the direction of the village. Recognizing them as scouts left to watch the rear, Dusty put aside his interest in the missing girl and walked over to where the men swung from their lathered horses.

"There's a bunch of Yankees on our trail, Cap'n Dusty," announced one of the pair, a grizzled corporal with surprisingly young eyes.

"How many, Vern?"

"Only ten—but they look to have one of our officers a prisoner."

"Ten!" Billy Jack grunted. "We've nothing to worry about there."

"Not if that's all there is," Dusty agreed.

"Which same I can't see any Yankee commander being fool enough to send just ten men after *us*," Billy Jack admitted dismally. "And I'd be plumb mortified if one sold us that low."

"We'd best take a look," Dusty stated. "Guidon, my horse!"

Already the company's guidon carrier had antici-
pated the command. It was his duty, in addition to carrying the company's identifying pennant, to hold and
tend to the commanding officer's mount. Fortunately
he had not placed the horse's feed bag on and swiftly
saddled the black ready for use. An able second-in-com-
mand, Red stood by Dusty's side, ready for orders.

"Form the men up ready," Dusty said while waiting
for his horse. "If we have to, we'll fall back and hold the
village."

"Yo!" Red replied.

Accompanied by Billy Jack, Dusty rode up the slope
but halted below the rim. A signal brought one of the
pickets to them, and Dusty handed over his black's
reins. Taking the field glasses from his saddle pouch,
Dusty went on foot until he could look cautiously over
the rim and present the approaching enemy with as
little chance as possible of locating him. He noted with
approval that his men each selected a concealed position and doubted if the enemy knew they had been
discovered.

Focusing his field glasses, Dusty first studied the distant body of men and then scoured the surrounding
area. He saw no sign of supporting troops following at a
distance behind the first party and brought his attention
to them once more. By that time they had come close
enough for him to study details, and what he saw puzzled him. While his scouts proved correct as to the number of the enemy and the presence of a Confederate
soldier, they erred in one detail.

"That's Cousin Buck with the Yankees," Dusty told
Billy Jack, having recognized Captain Buck Blaze,
Red's elder brother.

"A prisoner?" the sergeant major growled.

"If he is, they trust him plenty. He's still wearing his
guns."

A captured officer might, on being given his parole,

be permitted to retain his arms, but not when being escorted through hostile territory. Watching the men, a cold, almost clairvoyant feeling crept over Dusty. All too well he knew how badly the war went elsewhere for the Confederacy. Fighting ability and cold courage could not match the superior facilities of the Union, and the U.S. Navy's blockade of the South starved Dixie of the necessary materials that might otherwise have been imported from Europe. Maybe—

"I'm going to show myself, Billy Jack," he decided.

"Yo!" replied the noncom.

Rising, Dusty walked up onto the rim and stood in full view of the approaching party. Almost immediately they came to a halt and the officer at Buck Blaze's side turned to speak to him. Removing his campaign hat, Buck swung it over his head in a circle from right to left. Dusty relaxed and felt sure he guessed correctly at the reason for the party following him. If there had been danger, Buck would have swung his hat in the other direction; trusting that the Yankee did not know the meaning, to a Texan, of a "wave 'round." Waved from left to right, the hat signal meant "danger, steer clear."

Increasing their pace, the party rode closer. At fifty yards' distance they came to a halt.

"It's all right, Dusty!" Buck called, indicating the white flag carried by the Yankee guidon.

"I'll leave my escort here while we talk, Captain . . . Fog," the Yankee captain at Buck's side continued.

Captain Baines Hardy of the 6th New Jersey Dragoons wondered if he might be running into a trap. Could that small man be *the* Captain Dusty Fog who raided the Dragoons' camp and followed up a devastating attack by capturing a well-guarded Union army payroll?*

Riding closer, Hardy studied Dusty and, with a pro-

* Told in *The Colt and the Sabre.*

fessional soldier's eye, saw beneath the small exterior. Yes sir, small or tall as a pine tree, there stood a *man* capable of *all* feats attributed to Captain Fog.

"The war's over, Dusty," Buck said in a flat, emotionless voice as he and Hardy dismounted.

Despite having guessed the same thing, Dusty could not hold down his low-spoken, "Over!"

Breathing in deeply, Hardy waited for the next question, one he did not relish answering. It was one thing to stand in his regiment's mess and boast of having licked the rebs, but quite another to repeat the words when facing Captain Fog's company and backed by only ten men.

Of all the Confederate commands, the Army of Arkansas under Ole Devil Hardin had been the most consistently successful during the last eighteen months. On other fronts, the Union's superior equipment gave them an ascendancy. In Arkansas alone did the Confederacy maintain their record of victory, which had been established in the early days of the war.

So men of the Texas Light Cavalry would not accept Lee's surrender terms mildly. In fact some considerable concessions had been made by the Union's leaders when requesting Ole Devil's cessation of hostilities.

"General Hardin sent us after you, Captain," Hardy explained after being introduced. "The Union government wants to avoid the chance of . . . incidents."

"Which's why I came along, Dusty," Buck went on. "Uncle Devil said for you to report back to him right away."

"Not until I do what I came out here for," Dusty stated.

"The war's over, Captain," Hardy pointed out.

"It ended yesterday morning for those folks in the village," Dusty replied.

"How do you mean?"

"Hannah's guerrillas were there, Captain."

Stepping by Dusty, Hardy looked down the slope. He knew the village and its people, so a low growl left his lips. Fury showed on his face as he turned to Dusty.

"Hannah did it?"

"We reckon so. There's nobody left alive and that's always been his way."

"He's a reb—"

"Hannah's no Confederate," Dusty corrected. "He's like most guerrillas on both sides, a bloody-handed butcher out for loot. General Hardin's outlawed all of them and took time to hunt the bands down. As soon as we heard that Hannah was hereabouts, the general sent my company out after them."

Hooves drummed and the three officers turned to see Kiowa galloping up the slope toward them. Bringing his horse to a halt, the sergeant dropped from his saddle and threw Dusty as near a military salute as he ever achieved.

"The rain mussed up their sign some, but I reckon it can be followed," Kiowa said.

"Rest your horse," Dusty told him. "Billy Jack, tell Mr. Blaze we're pulling out as soon as the burial detail finishes its work."

"You're to return with me, Captain Fog," Hardy reminded.

"How about it, Buck?" asked Dusty.

Only for a moment did Buck Blaze hesitate, then replied, "I'm with you."

"Are you fixing to stop us, Captain?" Dusty said, looking at Hardy.

At first the Union officer did not answer. His eyes went to the ravaged village and he shook his head. "The hell I am. I'm coming with you."

2

HANNAH'S HIDEOUT

"One thing, Captain," Dusty said, before moving from where he stood. "Who's in command?"

That point had occurred to Hardy as he made the offer. However, there could be only one answer. Hardy might be older than Dusty and a career officer trained in the West Point Military Academy; the South may have lost the war, too, but he knew he rode with his master.

"I'm under your orders, Captain Fog."

"Can you trust your men?" asked Dusty. "I don't want any trouble."

"They're regular soldiers. I can trust them."

Men who made the army their career tended to be less vindictive than those enlisted under the stimulus of patriotism in time of war. For all that, Dusty watched the Yankees as they approached. He liked what he saw. Hard-bitten, tough, but disciplined was how they struck him, and the time served had given him the knack of knowing such things. While Hardy's men showed some professional interest, no hint of hostility came as they approached Dusty's company.

Assembling Company C, Dusty told them the news. A stunned silence followed his words. At last Billy Jack asked the question on every mind.

"Who-all won, Cap'n Dusty?"

"Nobody," Dusty replied. "They just got the good sense at last to call off the killing."

In a command that had suffered heavy losses and defeats or fought on its home ground, so saw enemy depradations on a personal level, the news might have been taken differently. Most of Dusty's men thought only of one thing. The end of the war meant they could return home to Texas and resume their interrupted lives.

"I'm still going after Hannah," Dusty went on. "Who's with me?"

"Can't rightly recollect you ever having to ask for volunteers afore, Cap'n Dusty," drawled the elderly corporal. "And until Ole Devil tells us different, we-all still under your command."

"Then have your food and we'll move when we've done what's needed here."

It said much for the chivalrous reputation gained by the Texas Light Cavalry in general and Company C in particular that none of Hardy's men connected them with the raid on the village. Nor did the Yankees make any comments on the outcome of the war. Like their officer, Hardy's men knew the value of discretion and did not feel it advisable to flaunt the Union's victory when faced with odds of around four to one.

Rebel and Yankee worked together in the grisly business of burying the dead, and their hatred of Hannah grew as each further atrocity was discovered. Even the older Texans, who had seen the results of Indian raids, felt sickened at what they saw. The fact that white men had been responsible for the massacre made its effect so much worse.

A wild-eyed Prince, recovered from Dusty's blows,

prowled disconsolately among the other men, searching in the wreckage and ruins, but finding no sign of the beautiful girl met on his previous visit. At last he stood at the edge of the houses and stared around. Hearing footsteps, he turned and found Dusty approaching.

"She's not here," Prince said.

"Could be she's away visiting kin," Dusty replied, hoping to hold out some faint hope to which the other might cling.

"No," Prince groaned. "All the kin she had in the world was right here. Why, she'd never been farther than Little Rock in her life."

"You must have known her pretty well," Dusty said.

"I never laid a hand on her—"

"And I never thought you did."

"Hell, Cap'n Dusty. She was different to any other gal I ever met," Prince groaned. "She was that pretty, had a face like an angel. We'd walk down by the creek, then sit and talk. How that gal'd talk. She hated being cooped up in this one-hoss li'l village and wanted to see some of the big cities she'd read about."

"She didn't care for it here, then?"

"What pretty gal would? If it hadn't been for the war, I'd've taken her out of it myself. In fact I damned near went over the hill for her."

"You made the right decision, Tracey," Dusty told him. "Not deserting, I mean—"

"If I'd done it—" Prince began.

"You'd've been hunted down and brought back. Which wouldn't've done either of you any good. You'd've been shot as a deserter and she couldn't've gone back to her folks after it."

"But she's either dead . . . or . . ."

"It looks that way."

"If Hannah's got her, I'll finish him, no matter where he goes!" Prince spat out.

"We'll maybe find out what happened to her," Dusty

replied. "Only when we catch up to Hannah's bunch, mind that you follow orders. If I see you making a wild move, I'll have you hawg-tied until it's over."

"I'll not forget, Cap'n," Prince promised.

"I know," Dusty replied. "Go get your horse. We'll be pulling out soon."

Grim-faced men took to their horses after the burial detail completed its work. With Kiowa ahead as lead scout, Company C started on what would be its last patrol together. Nobody spoke much as they rode. The somber nature of their business did not stimulate conversation, even if Dusty had permitted chatter when on the move in hostile territory. In addition to what they had seen in the village, the Texans rode with the knowledge that the war was over and gave thought to what the future might hold in store for them.

Shortly before sundown they made camp and spent a silent night, waiting for sufficient light to let them resume their journey. At dawn they fed, cared for the horses, and moved on again. Despite the rains, Kiowa managed to keep them on the trail and they covered mile after mile through the Arkansas hill country.

Accompanying Company C and studying them, Hardy could see how they built up their splendid record as military raiders. Only the fact that his escort were all veteran cavalrymen prevented them from slowing the Texans down. The average member of the Dragoons, volunteers from the East, could never have maintained such a pace. Never had Hardy seen such superb horse handling. Even the mules of the artillerymen did not slow down the party to any appreciable extent. Nor did the Texans allow speed to preclude caution. In addition to Kiowa, who needed to concentrate on reading tracks, two scouts rode ahead. A further pair rode on each flank and four more brought up the rear. Surrounded by that square of keen eyes, there would be little chance of any enemy surprising them.

All through the day they rode without a sight of Hannah's cutthroat band, although the tracks grew clearer. Apparently Hannah did not expect any pursuit, for he took no precautions to hide his party's sign. That figured, though. The area in which he traveled lay somewhat to the west of the main battle area and had been little touched by either side.

As night approached, the two lead scouts returned and reported to Dusty.

"Kiowa's done gone ahead, Cap'n," one said. "Allows he saw a smidgin of smoke rising and's gone to check on it."

"We'll make camp and wait for him at the next water," Dusty stated. "Where is it?"

"Maybe half a mile on," the scout answered.

Again the men made camp and prepared to spend another night under the stars. While the Yankees had brought along jerked meat and hardtack biscuits, they had the meager fare augmented by pemmican—that rare Indian delicacy*—offered by the Texans. In return the Dragoons shared out their coffee, an item that had recently been in very short supply in the blockade-starved ranks of the Texas Light Cavalry.

Toward midnight Hardy woke as voices came from close by. He sat and saw Kiowa had returned. The dark-faced scout squatted on his heels, a bowie knife in his hand. Watched by Dusty, Red, and Billy Jack, he used the knife's clipped point to draw a map on a patch of cleared and flattened earth.

"How does it look?" Hardy asked, joining the others.

"I've had easier chores," Dusty replied.

On looking down, Hardy found that Kiowa produced a pretty fair map; and he also agreed with Dusty's summing-up of the situation. The guerrillas' camp, consisting of seven buildings formed in a half circle, lay across

* The recipe for making pemmican is given in *Comanche*.

the bottom of a valley. An arrow indicated the line of march the attackers must take, and Hardy found they had to approach along the valley to reach the buildings.

"Kiowa allows that we can move on foot along the valley sides, but they'd be too steep for fancy horseback work," Dusty explained. "That circle on the far side of the cabins's their corral."

"What force has Hannah?" Hardy inquired.

"His own band runs at around thirty mostly, but likely men from some of the other guerrilla bunches we've bust up are with him. Kiowa reckons on thirty horses in the corral and at least that many again range-grazing out back of it."

"It doesn't follow there's a man for every horse, though."

"Nope."

"With your company and my men, we may have them outnumbered."

"Maybe," Dusty drawled. "Only they've the advantage of the ground."

"Then what do you mean to do, Captain?" asked Hardy.

"Move out now and try to reach that valley before daylight," Dusty answered. "If we do, we'll play it Indian style."

Knowing that Indians of various tribes showed a preference for making an attack during the first light of dawn—he had learned that in lectures at West Point—Hardy nodded his agreement.

"And if we don't make it in time?" he went on.

"Then we'll just have to play them as they fall," Dusty replied.

The first snag to Dusty's plan was that the mountain howitzer's mules could not be expected to tote their loads at speed through the darkness. Such a trip would be difficult enough for horses carrying skilled riders and practically impossible for the mules while burdened with the bulk of the dismantled gun or ammunition boxes. So Dusty told the artillerymen to follow at their best speed, leaving a corporal and four Texans to guide and protect his support armament.

Despite hard riding, plus some of the finest horse handling Hardy had ever seen, it soon became apparent that they would not reach their objective in time for a dawn rush, which might take the guerrillas by surprise while still in bed. So Dusty halted the column, told the men to rest their horses and themselves, and then went on foot with Kiowa to scout the enemy camp.

Dusty had not expected an easy time during the attack and as he lay in cover studying the valley, he knew he guessed right. Three log cabins, stoutly built and made for defense, curved on either side of the large building that faced toward Dusty across the valley bottom. From its appearance, the main building had been erected as a combination store and saloon. A lean-to stood at its right end and under this was a tarpaulin-draped object which Dusty could not identify, but felt looked vaguely familiar. At the other end of the main building, its reins fastened to a post, was a fine-looking horse, saddled and ready for use. On the building's porch sat a trio of bearded men, nursing muzzle-loading rifles, with revolvers and knives at their belts. None of them appeared to be taking their duties as guards too seriously, however, but they posed a serious problem.

"Not many of 'em stirring yet, Cap'n Dusty," Kiowa whispered.

"No," Dusty agreed. "If it wasn't for that bunch on the porch, we could still've made our charge."

"There's a couple by the corral," Kiowa said disgustedly. "Not more'n a quarter asleep, either. No sneaking up on *them*."

It had been Dusty's intention to have Kiowa pass around the buildings and turn loose the guerrillas' horses. In the face of the guards that would prove an impossibility.

"We'll leave it, then," Dusty decided.

"How about having that sharpshooter drop them jaspers on the porch?"

"I'd thought of it. But as soon as the first took lead, the other pair'd be up and running."

"Yeah," grunted Kiowa.

"So it looks like we have to do it the hard way," Dusty said. "Let's go."

Half an hour passed without any sign of stirring at the guerrilla camp. A couple of garishly dressed women appeared on the main building's porch and stood talking with the guard, but beyond that Dusty could see no change in the situation. Putting aside his thoughts of a mounted charge as being sure to alert the enemy, Dusty brought his men in on foot. Darting from cover to cover, keeping out of sight as well as possible, the Texans and Yankees drew ever closer to their objective. Three hundred yards still had to be covered before they reached the more open ground over which the last part of their advance must be made. However, if they managed to get that close undetected, they might bring off a surprise charge to demoralize the guerrillas and throw any defense into confusion.

Unfortunately that did not happen. Even as Dusty made his summing-up of the situation, the alarm was raised. Not by the guards. One of the women, looking out along the valley, saw signs of movement. Letting out a screech, she pointed and the guard looked up to see soldiers approaching. Lurching to his feet, one of the men threw up his rifle and fired a fast-taken shot. While it had no effect, the crack of exploding powder served to wake the guerrilla camp.

"Double march!" Dusty roared, knowing there to be no further need for silence or stealth.

In fact the sooner his men launched their attack, the

less chance of an organized defense was given to the enemy. From a stealthy walk, the men changed to a fast trot, although the nature of the valley sides did not lend itself to quick movement. The soldiers spread across the floor of the valley had a better chance and the men from the slopes tended to drift downward for easier going.

Already shouts from the buildings told of alarmed men, and soon rifle barrels began to appear at windows. With almost two hundred and fifty yards to cover, the muzzle-loading rifles did not pose too serious a threat, although bullets began to whistle through the air around the soldiers. Then Dusty saw something more deadly dangerous than the rifles.

Three men burst into sight from the side door and under the lean-to of the main building. Showing practiced speed, they sprang forward and stripped the tarpaulin from the thing that had earlier interested Dusty. What they exposed to view handed the small Texan a shock.

What appeared to be a flat tray was mounted on the wheels of an artillery carriage, and across the tray twenty-five metal tubes lined in the direction of the attackers, each holding a .58-caliber bullet ready to be vomited out in their direction. Asked what arms he might have expected to find among the guerrillas, Dusty would never have thought of a Billinghurst Requa Battery gun; yet one faced him, and already a hand tugged at its firing handle.

"Get down!" Dusty roared.

And not a moment too soon!

Down dropped the Requa's hammer, striking the waiting percussion cap. A tiny spurt of flame sparked into the train of gunpowder, which lay in a groove beneath the base of the cartridges. With a sullen rapid roaring, the barrels fired in turn, starting at the center and working outward on each side. Twenty-five bullets hissed through the air and formed a more deadly threat than any muzzle-loading rifle.

Two men, slower than their companions, each caught a bullet and crashed to the ground. The rest, having dived for cover at the sight of the gun and hearing Dusty's warning, avoided the deadly blast of the Requa. Which did not mean they were out of danger. Despite its clumsy appearance, given the right equipment and training, a skilled Requa crew could get off six or seven volleys a minute. From the way they moved, the trio behind the gun possessed all the requisites to keep up the top rate of fire.

Pulling on one of the levers that rose at the rear of the Requa, the gunner opened the breech. Already his companions held a magazine, a metal bar pierced at barrel-wide intervals with holes through which bullets were placed and held in position for insertion to the twenty-five breeches. After the gunner pulled out and discarded the fired magazine, his men slid its replacement into the holes. Then he ran a train of powder from his flask into the channel to ignite the bullets, and closed the breech. In something under ten seconds the Requa stood ready to turn loose another twenty-five death-dealing missiles.

The Requa Battery gun, an early attempt to produce a volume-of-fire weapon, had limitations in use. While the barrels could be moved laterally to spread the charge, their movement was necessarily limited. Nor could the gun be traversed unless the whole carriage be moved, which rendered it useless against a target that moved across its front. In wet weather the train of powder in the groove easily became soaked and inoperative; although that did not matter in the present case. In spite of its limitations, the Requa posted a serious problem to Dusty's men. The gun found its ideal conditions against a body of men advancing toward it along a fixed line—it was mostly used in defense of the narrow covered bridges that crossed most rivers in the eastern battle areas—and Dusty found his command in that unenviable position.

"Keep down and don't waste powder," he called. "How are they?"

"Denny's hurt bad," Billy Jack replied.

"This feller's dead," another Texan went on, kneeling by the side of the Yankee he had drawn to shelter.

"Do what you can for Denny," Dusty said. "Red, Captain Hardy, get your men moving into position. Keep well up on the slopes."

"Yo!" came two replies.

Gathering the men assigned to them, the two officers moved off to attend to their duties. By going well up the valley sides and keeping to cover, they made their way without loss around to where they could watch and cover the rear of the buildings. Each officer had men carrying shoulder arms, rifles of various types in Red's case, and Spencer carbines in the hands of the Yankees. The dead Union soldier reduced Hardy's party by one, but Dusty felt the seven-shot carbines of the others prevented the need of his sending a replacement.

A few shots at the rear of the building drove back those of the guerrillas who showed signs of trying to escape. Using a Spencer carbine looted from the Yankees, Red tumbled one of the corral guards and the other ran the gauntlet of fire to reach the main building in safety. Out on the range, the two men tending to the grazing remuda took in the situation and decided on flight. That reduced the guerrillas' chances of escape, but would only make them fight the harder.

With the rear bottled up, Dusty studied the buildings. Some shots came from them, but his men wasted no powder in replying. His eyes took in the horse tethered by the rear door and he knew what he must do. Only one man among the guerrillas rated the special consideration of having his horse so close to hand. By his cold-blooded disregard for human life and willingness to kill as a means of ending opposition, Hannah could take such a precaution. If he reached that powerful animal, he had the means of escape; and of all the guerrillas, Hannah was the man Dusty wanted most. So, much as he hated the idea, Dusty reached a decision.

"Thad! Thad Baylor!" he yelled.

"Yo!" replied the sharpshooter.

"Kill that horse by the main building."

A hundred yards behind the attackers, Thad Baylor settled himself down to do his work. Placing the barrel of his heavy rifle on his folded jacket, which rested upon a rock selected as being just the right height, Baylor cuddled its butt into his shoulder. He closed his left eye and focused the other through the telescope sight. Close by his hand lay a range-finding stadium; a brass plate with a sliding bar that ran up a graduated scale. Fixed to the bottom of the stadium, a twenty-five-inch cord enabled its user to hold the plate at exactly the right distance from the eye while he studied his target through the hole in the brass and adjusted the bar to learn what distance separated them.

With that rifle, made by his own hands—Baylor was a skilled gunsmith whose deadly accurate shooting brought employment as a special-duty sniper—he could hit a man at seven hundred yards. The horse stood no more than five hundred yards away an offered a larger target.

Satisfied with his aim, Baylor squeezed the trigger, watched the side hammer drop on to the percussion cap, and felt the solid jar of the recoil against his shoulder. Through the cloud of whirling powder smoke, he saw the horse collapse, kicking wildly, and then go still.

Dusty nodded in cold satisfaction. That put Hannah

in the same position as his men, without a horse on which he might make an escape.

"And now all we have to do is fetch them out," the small Texan mused.

3

FREE PASSAGE FOR THE WOMEN

"The gun's got here, Cap'n Dusty!" called one of the soldiers.

Turning, Dusty saw that the mountain howitzer's party had wisely halted beyond rifle range.

"Keep them penned in, Billy Jack," he ordered, and moved back from his position to dart away in the direction of the howitzer.

Dusty's way lay by Baylor, and he found the sharpshooter going through the tricky business of reloading the rifle. Halting to pass on orders, Dusty sat down in cover and waited until the other finished.

To make the most of the rifle's accuracy potential, a sharpshooter did not just tip powder down the barrel and ram home a ball on top. Baylor slid a brass tube into the barrel of his rifle, then tipped a carefully measured amount of gunpowder down it. In that way he ensured that none of the powder grains lodged in the rifling but all arrived at the chamber. Removing the tube, he slipped the rifle's false muzzle from a pocket, fitting it into place.

Before rifling the barrel, when making the rifle, Baylor turned down its muzzle slightly and carefully cut off the last two inches. The cut-off portion was fitted with four pins, and holes to correspond with them were drilled into the end of the barrel. With that done, barrel and false muzzle received their rifling grooves and the mouth of the latter was reamed out slightly to make "starting" the bullet easier. Using a false muzzle ensured the correct seating of the bullet—which was slightly larger than the bore size, although smaller than that of bore and rifling grooves, to make for a gas-tight seal and extra power—and protected the true muzzle from wear or damage, which would spoil the rifle's fine accuracy.

After fixing on the false muzzle, Baylor placed home a carefully molded, sized and weighted bullet. Nor did his attentions end there. Next, he fitted a bullet starter over the end of the false muzzle, moving down its piston until the prepared cavity fitted over the head of the bullet. A firm tap thrust home the piston and drove the bullet down into the barrel proper. Putting aside the starter, Baylor finished seating the bullet with his ramrod.

"I want that Requa silenced, Thad," Dusty said as the man placed a percussion cap on its nipple. "Only don't fire until I tell you. Then drop the gunner."

"Yo!" Baylor answered.

He hated the work his shooting skill brought, but the sights at the ravaged village made him feel less sympathy than usual with his victims. Settling down to rest his rifle again, he made sure that the barrel could line on the Requa's gunner. Finding it would do so, he waited for the order to shoot.

Having made use of Baylor's special skill before, Dusty knew the other's feelings on the subject of long-range selective killing. So the small Texan did not want to delay for too long and give Baylor a chance to brood. One small consolation came as Dusty realized that, with the war over, Baylor should be able to return to working as a gunsmith and stop killing.

Things were not to work out so easily for Baylor, and at a future date Dusty would once again find himself asking the sharpshooter to use his skill to take a human life.*

Leaving Baylor, Dusty made his way to the rear. Twice bullets hissed by the small Texan's head, and once lead churned the dirt under his feet, but he reached his support weapon without injury.

By the time Dusty arrived, the howitzer's crew had already assembled their piece and the sergeant stood waiting for orders for its use.

"Loaded with shell, Cap'n," the noncom announced.

"Reckon you can hit the buildings from here?" asked Dusty.

"Once we get the range."

"You've only got thirty-two rounds, sergeant," Dusty pointed out, nodding to the four narrow boxes standing to the rear after being unloaded from the two ammunition mules. "A half pound exploding charge's not all that powerful, so we'll have none to spare if we need to handle all six cabins and the big place."

"Reckon not, sir," admitted the sergeant, surprised that a cavalry officer, even Captain Dusty Fog, should know so much about artillery matters.

A howitzer was designed to throw its shell in a high arc and could not be depressed for level fire. While ideal for lobbing its charges over obstacles, it did not offer extreme accuracy of the kind Dusty required.

"Could you tilt the stock up on a rock and bring the barrel into line that way?" Dusty inquired.

"Not without risking busting something," the sergeant replied.

"The war's over," Dusty reminded him. "Let the Yan-

* Told in *Wagons to Backsight*.

kees worry about repairing any damage if they want the gun."

"Now me, I'd never've thought of that," grinned the sergeant. "Which's likely why I never made captain." He looked around and pointed to the left. "Lay hold and haul her to that flat rock there, boys."

Springing to the howitzer, the four-man crew moved it into the position indicated by their sergeant. By resting the stock of the trail upon the top of the rock, they tilted the barrel down so that it pointed toward the buildings. Taking up his position behind the gun, the sergeant looked along its thirty-nine-inch tube and gave orders to the number-three man.

"Trail right," said the sergeant, and the man swung the trail in the required direction. "Trail left. A touch more. Steady!"

Setting down the trail, the number-three took the vent pick from his pocket, inserted it down the vent, pierced the cloth of the cartridge, and exposed its powder ready for the primer. After fastening his lanyard to the primer, the number-two man slipped the primer into the vent and stepped aside.

"Fire!" barked the sergeant, looking toward the target.

A tug on the lanyard and the howitzer jerked as its powder charge ignited. Its recoil slid the trail back across the rock, but no damage occurred. From where he stood, Dusty could see the flight of the shell. Like a black streak, it converged with, then struck the wall of the main building by the door and bust through. No explosion followed and the sergeant gave a low, disgusted grunt.

"Damned Borman fuses," he snorted. "We should ought to complain to the Ordnance Department."

"Ours, or the Yankees'?" asked Dusty, for the fuses probably came from raids on the enemy.

"There's that," admitted the sergeant. "Give her half a second less on the next one, Ezra."

"Yo!" answered the number-two man, who served as ammunition carrier and fuse cutter.

"Do you get any misfires?" Dusty asked.

"That depends on the fuses, but we get a few every time there's sustained fire," the sergeant replied, watching the loading and checking that the fuse had been cut correctly.

Working with practiced speed, the crew loaded their piece and lined it again. Whether the reduction of burning time affected things, or the fuse functioned better than its predecessor, on the second try the shell passed through the wall and burst inside the big building.

Without needing further orders, the men went through the reloading routine. The number-one man sponged out the tube, then rammed home the charge. Before they completed their work, an interruption came.

"White flag from the big cabin, Cap'n Dusty!" yelled Billy Jack.

Although Dusty could see the flag, he felt puzzled. It hardly seemed likely that Hannah's band would surrender so easily, knowing their fate for the attacker on the small village. Yet none of the guerrillas fired as he walked back toward the men. The big building's front door opened and a woman came out. Carrying the white flag over her shoulder, she advanced toward the Texans.

"Keep down, all of you!" Dusty barked as the woman shouted something to the occupants of the other cabins. Then, as she drew nearer, he went on, "Hold it there."

Obediently the woman came to a halt. Nobody would ever regard her as beautiful, or even good-looking. She stood maybe five foot nine, with a muscular development many a man might envy. Rawboned, with few of the feminine curves that attract male admiration, she wore a plain riding habit and white blouse. Her inscrutable face told nothing, but her eyes flickered glances about her, while a large nose hooked over a rattrap mouth and rock-hard jaw.

"I want to talk to your boss," she declared in a harsh, rasping voice.

"I'm in command here," Dusty informed her. "Speak your piece."

"Why, for you abusing us poor folks I—"

"If that's all you have to say, turn 'round and head back," the small Texan interrupted. "You *know* why we're here."

"You fixing to stay on and fetch us out, no matter how long it takes?"

All the time she spoke, the woman continued to look around. If a man had stood before him, Dusty would have suspected the other was studying the situation and assessing the danger. Maybe that was why Hannah sent out a woman, figuring she could look around without arousing suspicion. A shrewd move, if correct, provided she knew enough to appreciate fully what she saw.

"That's why we're here," he told her.

"We've a tolerable strong place down there, soldier boy," the woman warned, nodding to the cabins.

"And you're stuck in it," Dusty replied. "There're three more companies and a battery of Whitworth rifles not far behind and coming fast."

Clearly the woman understood that Dusty used the term "rifles" when meaning Whitworth rifled cannon. Through the war, the British-built Whitworth "rifles" gained a reputation for accuracy far exceeding that of any smooth-bore cannon. While a Confederate artillery battery rarely had more than four guns, as opposed to the Union army's six, that number could speedily reduce the cabins to rubble, and at a range beyond which any shoulder rifle or the Requa might reach them.

"There's women in the big cabin," the woman said after a brief pause.

"Prisoners?" The word cracked from Dusty's lips before he could stop it.

"Sure," she replied, just a shade too quickly.

"You're a liar. Hannah never takes prisoners."

"There's still women down there," the woman insisted. "You aiming to start shooting with 'em inside?"

"What's on your mind?"

"Let me go down and fetch the gals out."

Having already been thinking about the women he knew accompanied most guerrilla bands, Dusty saw an answer to his problem. Certainly leaving them in the cabin would seriously impede his handling of the situation. So he gave his agreement to the woman's proposal.

"All right. Go fetch them out. I'll give you no more than fifteen minutes to do it."

"That'll be long enough."

"It'd better be!" Dusty snapped. "While you're convincing the women, let the men know how things stand. After you've brought the gals out and clear, any man who wants can follow as long as he comes with his hands in the air and no weapons on him. I'll see they get a fair trial."

Not a great inducement to surrender, as Dusty knew, for no court would show mercy to the ravagers of the Quaker village. However he had to make the offer and hope that some of the guerrillas would accept it.

"I'll tell 'em," promised the woman, and turned to walk back toward the cabins. Before entering the main building, she stood for a moment and spoke to the occupants of the cabins; but the words did not reach Dusty's ears.

Immediately on the woman's departure, Dusty threw a look around and yelled an order for his men to keep in cover. Some of them had exposed themselves to gain a better view of what happened and made entirely too

good targets for his liking. While Dusty respected a flag
of truce he doubted whether the guerrillas possessed
such scruples. Taking out his watch, he checked on the
time and hoped that the women would agree to accept
his offer of free passage and come out. If they did not, he
must do his duty and they take their chances in the
ensuing fighting.

"What the hell!" Dusty growled after sending his guidon carrier and another man up the slopes so that they
could carry word of his arrangements to the parties
covering the rear of the buildings.

Darting from cover to cover, Tracey Prince flung
himself the remaining yards to land at Dusty's side.
None of the other men had moved, keeping in cover
and not indulging in the kind of horseplay less disciplined troops would at such a time.

"Did she say if they'd any prisoners in there, Cap'n
Dusty?" Tracey asked.

Until that moment, being so busy with the organization of the attack and other details, Dusty had almost
forgotten Prince and the girl "with a face like an angel."

"She tried a bluff, but called if off," Dusty replied.

"Then Rowena's not with them?"

"If she was, that woman'd've mentioned it. They'd
not miss playing an ace in the hole like that."

"I reckon not," admitted Prince disconsolately. "But
she wasn't at the village, we know that."

"It's almost four months since you were there, Tracey," Dusty pointed out. "Could be that she left during
that time."

"Sure, Cap—"

"Women coming out of the cabin, Cap'n Dusty!"
called one of the men.

Shooting out a hand, Dusty hauled Prince back behind the shelter of the rock.

"You stay down and act sensible, Tracey," the small

Texan warned. "Those jaspers down there can't be trusted."

When sure the other would obey, Dusty peered around the rock. Already half a dozen women gathered before the main building and more left the cabins. Fifteen in all stood in a small group and the woman who organized their escape spoke rapidly to them. With that done, she led the rest in the direction of the attackers; nor did any of the camp followers show reluctance at leaving their men.

"They look in a tolerable hurry, Cap'n Dusty," Billy Jack commented.

"Likely figure that some of the men might have second thoughts and try to fetch them back," Dusty replied, then turned to the man at his side. "Keep down, damn you, Tracey."

"She's not with 'em!" Prince stated, and settled back into cover again. "Can I ask questions when they get here?"

"After the att—" Dusty began.

Suddenly there came from the main building a loud roar of exploding gunpowder. A brilliant, fiery, flaring glow showed even in the daylight while black smoke, flying timbers, and pieces of human bodies rose into the air. Caught in the blast of the explosion, the women were flung to the ground and the adjacent cabins suffered damage. The cabins on either side of the main building collapsed as their closest wall caught the force of the blast and roofs caved in. Where the big main building had stood, only a smoking crater remained.

"What the hell!" Dusty spat out. "If that gunner opened fire . . ."

Before he finished, Dusty realized that no half-pound exploding charge of a twelve-pounder howitzer shell could have wreaked such havoc. Yet there did not seem to be any alternative as a cause of the explosion.

Rising to their feet, the women started to stagger in

the direction of Dusty's men. Fortunately they had been far enough away to avoid the worst of the blast and, apart from damage to their clothing or grazed skin caused by being thrown to the ground, none appeared to be hurt.

"Just keep coming!" Dusty ordered. "And keep your hands in plain sight."

Women they might be, but those harridans from the guerrilla band would be as dangerous as rattlesnakes if they got among his men with the intention of making trouble. Dusty knew that his men would hesitate to open fire on women, even should the women hold weapons; or at least they might delay their actions that vital instant too long. So he aimed to take no chances.

"We'll have to watch 'em, Cap'n Dusty," Billy Jack stated, showing his mind ran on the same lines as his commanding officer's.

"Have Vern and four of the oldest married men do it," Dusty replied.

"You want them gals searched?"

"Watch 'em's all. Take them off to one side and well clear of the howitzer."

It seemed highly unlikely that the guerrillas would try such a desperate game as sending out their women with orders to jump the howitzer's crew after being passed through the attacking circle, but Dusty did not intend to take the chance. If some unfortunate circumstance deprived him of the howitzer's support, taking the cabins would be even more difficult. Even with the gun it was no feather bed. Without the howitzer to batter down walls and soften resistance, the guerrillas might hold out for a long time and take many lives before being overrun.

The women came closer and their leader glared wildly at Dusty. "You started shooting!" she accused.

"No, ma'am," Dusty replied.

"Then . . . then it must have been the gunpowder in the cellar."

"Gunpowd . . . ," Dusty started. "How much?"

"W-Hannah looted a Yankee supply column and got two wagonloads of it just afore Old Devil Hardin put out that order for us to quit."

Two wagonloads of gunpowder would be ample to cause such an explosion. Any number of things might have sparked it off. Careless handling, a chance mishap, bad management, might have supplied the means of ignition. Undisciplined guerrillas would take none of the necessary precautions to avoid accidents. One flicker of naked flame, even as small as a spark kicked by a boot nail, finding its way to the powder would be enough. From there a sympathetic explosion did the rest, running from keg to keg in split-seconds until the whole consignment went up.

Already shots came from the remaining buildings and bullets whistled through the air around the women. It almost seemed that the men in the cabins shot at their erstwhile companions and bed-mates.

"Get moving along the valley, you women!" Dusty barked. "Open fire, men!"

At his side, Prince half rose so as to speak with the women. Caught in the shoulder by a bullet from the cabins, the young soldier screamed and crashed down again.

"See to him, Billy Jack!" Dusty ordered. "Vern, get your bunch and herd the women off to the right side."

Showing his usual efficiency, Billy Jack had gathered up an escort of married, older men who would be less susceptible to female wiles. Certainly none of the selected escort showed any great interest in the disheveled women.

"Come on!" ordered the old corporal. "Do what the cap'n says and there'll be no trouble."

"Don't take any chances, or manhandle them in any way unless you have to," Dusty warned.

"Trust us for that, Cap'n Dusty," Vern replied. "Get moving, darlings, afore some of your friends down there shoot you by mistake."

Obediently enough, the women moved off and the corporal's party followed at a safe distance. With one responsibility lifted, Dusty turned his thoughts to taking the remainder of the guerrilla band. If Hannah had been in the main building, as seemed most likely, Dusty did not need to worry further about him.

4

THE ATTACK

Studying the ground ahead of him, Dusty doubted if the cabin on either side of the destroyed main building could offer much resistance. He heard faint screams of pain or cries for help coming from beneath the shattered framework and saw two men dragging themselves painfully from under the collapsed walls. However, the volume of fire that came from the remaining four cabins warned him that their occupants were still full of fight. Calling on the guerrillas to surrender at that point would be both futile and dangerous to the man who made the attempt.

"Gunner!" he yelled, cupping his hands around his mouth and seeing a wave to show that the other heard him. "Give the first cabin on the right a shot."

"Yo!" came the reply.

A skilled technician, the artillery sergeant did not give the order to open fire until he made sure of his aim. After taking such adjustments as he considered necessary, he stepped clear so as to observe the fall of the shot and barked the command to shoot. Banging loud, the howitzer sent its shell streaking away to pass through the wall of the desired cabin and burst inside.

Dusty could guess at the effect of the exploding charge in the confines of the cabin. Maybe the shell's comparatively weak load of powder could not blow up the building, but the blast and flying fragments of metal casing ought to have a highly demoralizing effect and do some physical damage. The cabins, proof against ordinary bullets, had not been constructed to withstand artillery bombardment from even a small mountain howitzer and would offer little protection to the men within. Faced by such a weapon, they must try to silence it or surrender.

"How's Tracey?" Dusty asked as he turned to look back at the howitzer again.

"Lucky," replied Billy Jack, kneeling by the still form of the soldier. "The bullet went through without hitting bone. I had to put him to sleep, but he's resting easy enough now."

"See to him," Dusty said, and prepared to call for a change of aim.

Before the words could be uttered, Dusty saw the number-one man of the gun's crew drop his rammer, then stagger and fall to the ground. Knowing that the man had been shot, Dusty first turned and looked toward the captive women. Certainly none of them could have done the shooting, for they sat quietly on the ground with their backs to the howitzer and watched by the corporal's guard.

Of course a chance bullet from the cabins might have dropped the soldier, but Dusty did not believe in taking chances. His eyes raked the cabins and saw only the barrels of rifles or carbines aimed in the direction of his party. On the second examination, however, he observed a sinister sight. The rifle that attracted his attention crept into view at the corner of the left outer cabin's second window and remained for a long time without firing. Then it barked and Dusty swung around in time to see the sergeant leap away from the howitzer. Not that Dusty needed such added confirmation, having recognized the barrel of a rifle just as specialized as the one Thad Baylor used. Clearly the guerrillas had a sharpshooter among them and he had used his skill to end the menace of the howitzer.

Equally obviously, that sharpshooter must be silenced before he wiped out the gun's crew. Dusty could not expect those artillerymen to stand exposed to fire and continue working their piece. Even if they did so, their accuracy must suffer, and there were few enough shells to handle the work ahead.

"Thad!" Dusty yelled. "There's a sharpshooter in the outer cabin on the left. He's going for the howitzer's crew."

"Yo!" Baylor answered, and moved his rifle into a firing position.

At first Baylor failed to locate the man, although he allowed for the time needed to go through the reloading procedure with a sharpshooter's rifle. Then he swung the rifle's barrel, eye behind the telescope sight watching the front of the building until he reached the outer window. Like the artillery sergeant, Baylor was a skilled technician and knew his work. If he had been in the enemy sharpshooter's place, he would not have remained in the same firing position if given the choice.

Sure enough, the barrel of the other sharpshooter's rifle stuck out of the second window, and Baylor could see its user kneeling behind it. Taking careful aim, Baylor squeezed the set trigger of his rifle. He fired just an instant before the other man, but soon enough. Caught in the chest by Baylor's bullet, the guerrilla jerked backward and tipped his rifle's barrel into the air, where its bullet went harmlessly flying.

"Got him!" Dusty said. "I don't think they'll have another man who can use that rifle."

True, any of the guerrillas could handle *a* rifle, but not to take advantage of the special accuracy offered by their dead sharpshooter's weapon. Baylor knew his work well enough to keep on watch and deal with anybody in the cabin who tried to use the dead man's rifle; so the bombardment could be resumed unhindered.

Despite the loss of one man, the howitzer could be kept in operation. Firing-drill instructions provided exercises by a diminished crew—even down to the ominous "service by two men" in case the remainder should be wiped out through enemy action—so the number-two man also assumed his dead companion's duties.

Again and again the howitzer banged sending its shells over the heads of Dusty's party and toward the cabins. Not all the shells hit the mark. A combination of short tube and poor sights did not make for accuracy at a range of six hundred yards. So three shells fell short and a couple more passed over the cabins: and not all which flew true exploded on arrival. However the destruction of the main building and disablement of the cabin on either side of it gave the howitzer's crew a surplus of ammunition which offset the necessary wastage.

It could not last. Finding their shelter under bombardment from beyond any range where their arms might hope to hit, such guerrillas as could gave thought to flight. The right-side outer cabin's rear door flew open and four men broke out to make a dash for the corral. Seeing the defection of their companions, more and more of the men in the remaining cabins took their chances on reaching the corral.

On the rear slopes, Red and Hardy ordered their men to shoot. However, only Red among the Texans held a repeater and one volley saw his men holding empty guns. Rather than take the time to reload, Red rose from his place. Twisting his hands back around the butts of his Colts, he drew the weapons.

"Come on, Texas Light!" he shouted. "Let's take 'em!"

Roaring their agreement, his men followed him in a rush down the slope and toward the front of the corral. Hardy only hesitated for a moment before launching his blue-clad section downward to support the Texans.

Not wishing to have the howitzer out of ammunition before effecting the destruction of the enemy's shelter, Dusty automatically counted the number of shots it fired. At each successive hit he expected to see either surrender flags or the guerrillas trying to escape. In the latter case, they would go by the rear doors and head for the corral. When the rush finally came, Dusty guessed how Red would react. Counting on his cousin to run true to form, Dusty had made his plans ready.

"Cease fire with the gun!" he yelled, waving his hat to attract the artillery sergeant's attention. "Bugler, sound the charge!"

Every man in Dusty's party had been expecting the order and discarded their shoulder arms so that they could have the advantage offered by their Colt revolvers. Even as Red led his men down the slope, he and they heard the wild, ringing notes of the bugle and recognized the call being blown. Bounding down the slope, the Texans held their fire until sure they could aim in the hope of hitting. Lead tore around them as the guerrillas cut loose, but none of it found a mark on human flesh.

Swarming forward in a fast, yet orderly rush, Dusty's men swept toward the front of the buildings. They expected little or no opposition from that direction and met none at first. Then, twenty yards from the nearest cabin, Dusty saw a shape appear at a window. Up came a rifle, lining in his direction. It would be ironic, he mused while throwing his left-hand Colt up into line, if he should be shot on his last assignment and after the end of the war. Thinking did not influence either Dusty's speed or aim. Still running, he fired, saw flame spurt from the guerrilla's rifle, and felt his hat spin backward to be halted when its storm strap snapped tight on his throat. Caught in the neck by Dusty's bullet, the guerrilla pitched back and fell out of sight. . . .

Reaching the cabin's door, Dusty found it had been weakened by a shell driving through the center. A kick sent it flying open inward and the small Texan went through fast. Although he entered the room ready to shoot, Dusty found no need to use his guns. The man by the window had been too badly lamed to escape and now lay dying on the floor. Looking around, Dusty saw the devastation caused in the living room by exploding shells. Torn, shattered bodies were scattered around and blood oozed stickily underfoot. With relief he saw no women among the bodies.

A sound from one of the other rooms sent Dusty across the charnel house the shells had created. Thrusting open a door, he found a guerrilla trying to escape. Despite having lost a foot during the bombardment, the man used a shotgun for a crutch and tried to hobble through the rear door.

"Hold it!" Dusty snapped.

With an almost bestial snarl of rage, the guerrilla turned and rammed his shoulder against the doorjamb to remain erect. Then he began to raise the shotgun. Dusty would have tried to take the man alive if he had held any other kind of weapon, but not when threatened by a shotgun's spreading charge. Much as he hated to do it, Dusty threw a shot with his right-hand Colt and drove the bullet into the man's head. Propelled through the door under the impact, the guerrilla triggered off a wild shot. Dusty heard the solid "whomp!" of lead striking the wall by his side. It had been a close thing. So close that the nearest of the buckshot balls pierced the timbers less than an inch from his side.

A savage struggle raged outside the cabin. Clearly the guerrillas had no intention of surrendering to the soldiers. Nor did the Texans hesitate to shoot to kill when doing so might easily cost them their own lives.

Leaping to the corral, one of the guerrillas threw down the top pole of its gate. He saw Red, ahead of the others, drawing close and spun around to snatch the revolver from his belt. Skidding to a halt, Red fired his right-hand Colt by instinctive alignment. Although the bullet hit the guerrilla, it neither killed him nor made him drop his gun. Without hesitation Red thumped off a shot from his left-hand gun. Again lead ripped into the guerrilla and he collapsed, the revolver sliding from limp fingers. Only then did Red turn his attention from the man.

Only fifteen guerrillas avoided injury during the bombardment and broke from the cabins. Caught between the two parties from the rear slopes and Dusty's advancing soldiers, they fought and died to a man. Hard-bitten veterans like the men of Company C had fought through the war, seeing much action and learning lessons. All knew better than to take chances and, like Red, had sense enough to continue firing if the enemy showed fight. When the shooting ended and the smoke blew from the scene, it appeared that the ravaged village had been completely avenged.

Grim-faced sections went into the remaining cabins, searching rooms and on two occasions being forced to kill wounded men who showed fight. At last not a living male member of Hannah's guerrilla band remained.

"Call them off, Red," Dusty ordered quietly, holstering his Colts and looking around.

"Yo!" Red replied "Bugler, sound recall."

As the notes of the bugle call rang out, Dusty gave his attention to other details that must be handled.

"Did we lose many, Red?"

"Dutchy Schmidt went under as we came down the slope," Red replied. "I don't know about any more, but I saw at least one get hit by the corral."

"Go look around," Dusty said.

Coming over, Hardy extended his hand. Admiration showed on the Yankee officer's face as he looked at Dusty.

"My congratulations, Captain Fog. You handled this whole affair very well."

"Thanks," Dusty answered. "Did you have any casualties?"

"Two men wounded, none killed."

Regarded in cold-blooded soldier logic, the whole affair had been very well managed. Taking and destroying a well-armed, desperate band of trained fighting men for so small a loss required ability, planning, and some small amount of luck. Due to Dusty's foresight, the guerrillas' strong camp became their deathtrap. Without the sharpshooter along, Hannah might easily have escaped on his waiting horse. In the absence of the mountain howitzer, only a long siege could have overcome the enemies' defenses. More than that; during the siege, which would have lasted for days, some of the guerrillas might have escaped during darkness. As it was, thanks to Dusty's planning, the entire band met its just end.

"It's a pity about Hannah," Hardy commented, nodding to the crater where the main building had been.

"Yep," agreed Dusty. "He's the one I wanted. Still, I reckon he's done for sure, don't you?"

"He's dead, even if he wasn't in the main building there," Hardy replied. "I wonder what caused the explosion?"

"Likely we'll never know," Dusty said. "Unless the women have an idea, that is."

"They were outside when it happened," Hardy pointed out.

"Sure," Dusty drawled. "Only I have to ask them about the gal from the village, so I might as well learn all I can."

Leaving Red to handle the business of attending to the wounded, Dusty and Hardy walked back by the cabins and toward where the women sat. Dusty frowned as he saw that only the old corporal and one man stood watch over the female prisoners. Seeing his commanding officer approaching, the corporal came to meet Dusty. Contrition showed on the noncom's seamed, leathery face as he halted and threw a smarter salute than usual.

"What's up, Vern?" Dusty asked.

"That big gal who did the talking for Hannah's lit out."

"Escaped?" Hardy growled.

"You might say that," Vern answered dryly, for he saw no reason to apologize to a Yankee officer.

"How'd it happen?" Dusty snapped.

"No excuse, Cap'n," Vern replied, stiffening to a brace.

"Which's no answer, either," Dusty pointed out.

"It was all my fault."

"I'm not blaming anybody else."

"Well, Cap'n, it was like this," Vern said. "Them gals settled down as good and peaceable as you like. Not a sign of fuss. So we started watching what went on at the cabins and—"

"When you got back to doing your duty, she'd gone," Dusty finished.

"That's about the size of it," admitted Vern. "I sent two of the boys to see if they can find her."

"Which they haven't," Dusty growled, nodding to where the soldiers returned. "Kiowa!"

"Yo!" answered the scout, and came over to Dusty's side.

"We lost one, see if you can trail her."

"I'll make a whirl at it," Kiowa promised, and slouched away.

After looking around him at the rough, broken country, Dusty put aside his thoughts of organizing a search should Kiowa fail. To do the job properly would take all his men and most likely have no success.

Swinging back toward the women, Dusty studied them. He noticed that all but one looked scared. Maybe they expected to be punished for their friend's desertion. If so, the exception to the rule showed little fear. Seated a little clear of the others, she met his gaze with defiance and a hint of mockery. Her age would be around Dusty's own and she kept it well. Tawny hair, unkempt in a reckless and somehow attractive manner framed a beautiful face. Blue eyes looked with no hint of meekness from under long lashes, and her full lips parted in a provocative manner to show firm white teeth.

As Dusty drew near her, the girl rose in a lithe, sinuous move. Under the cheap dress she wore lay a body rich and sensual. She knew just how to show it off to its best advantage.

"Why'd she run?" Dusty demanded.

Before replying, the girl glanced at her companions. It almost seemed that she flashed a message to them and none offered to speak or do more than raise their eyes to meet the small Texan's gaze.

"I reckon she didn't like the company, soldier boy," the girl said at last.

"And you do?"

"I can take or leave it."

"How about the rest of you women?" Hardy inquired.

"They're like me," the girl put in. "Don't care for walking."

"Let them speak for themselves," Dusty ordered.

"Maybe they've got nothing to say," answered the girl.

"And you have?"

A slow smile crept over the girl's lips and she winked. "Whyn't you-all take me off someplace quiet and find out?"

Almost two years of soldiering had given Dusty the opportunity to know a number of women and had worn away the callow edges of youth quicker than might have happened back home in Texas. Yet he could not hold down a slight flush of embarrassment as he heard the sniggers of the other women. The sound caused him to react quickly and, as it proved, in the best way to gain his ends.

"How'd you like for me to have two or three of the men take you off somewheres quiet?" he countered, and saw the flicker of fear that passed across the girl's face. "Sit down again!"

Slowly the girl sank to the ground and sat with her arms clasped around her knees. For some reason the threat held terror for her. Understandable when considering her age, but not in view of the company she kept. Dusty decided to follow up his advantage and learn all he could.

"Which of you were at the Quaker village?" he snapped. "And don't lie. I know that some of you were."

"I was, for one," the girl replied. "Only I didn't go until all the fuss was over."

"Why'd Hannah jump them?" Hardy put in.

"For loot. Why else?"

Clearly the girl felt puzzled at finding rebel and Yankee soldiers working together in amity. Her eyes went from Dusty to Hardy and back as she spoke.

"Damn it, girl!" Hardy barked. "Those Quakers had nothing—"

"They'd all got money," the girl corrected. "Real Yankee gold that'd be good no matter who won the war. That's what Hannah went after."

"And prisoners?" asked Dusty.

"Hell no," the girl answered. "Why'd we take prisoners, soldier boy? They'd have nobody to pay ransom for 'em."

"So you took nobody from the village?" Dusty said.

"No."

"Not even a real pretty li'l gal with blond hair?"

"No . . . ," the girl began, then a grin twisted her lips. "So that's where Handsome Jack we—"

"Go on," Dusty encouraged as the girl once more chopped off her words.

"I don't know a thing," the girl answered sullenly.

"Corporal!" Dusty snapped. "Go ask some of the men if they feel like having a mite of fun."

Once again the threat brought abut the desired result. For a moment the girl tried to show defiance, but that extra fear lurked behind it. Running her tongue tip over her lips, she shook her head.

"All right," she hissed. "Handsome Jack went into the village a day ahead of us. He was to learn if everything'd be set for us to follow. Only he never showed and Hannah got riled. Took the boys in without waiting. It seems like Handsome Jack eloped with the head preacher's daughter. I've never seen Hannah so potboiling wild—"

"You said you didn't go into the village until after it was over," Dusty growled.

"I heard the boys talking about it afterward."

"And this Handsome Jack jasper took off with the girl?"

"The night afore we hit," confirmed the girl.

With such a long start there would be no hope of following the man and girl's tracks. Dusty wondered if perhaps the girl's fate might be better than it appeared on the surface. From what he had heard about the blond girl, she could have gone willingly with the handsome stranger. Possible the man called Handsome Jack retained enough shreds of decency to want to save the girl from the kind of treatment Hannah's bunch handed out to female prisoners. It was a small hope, but all Dusty could offer to Prince when the soldier recovered consciousness.

There were other aspects of the affair which Dusty must attend to, so he put aside his thoughts of the abducted blond girl.

"Was Hannah in the big place when it blew up?" he asked.

"Where else?" countered the girl.

"Do you know what caused the explosion?"

"How could I?"

"How about the rest of you women?"

"Now, how the hell would they know?" scoffed the girl. "We all got out fast when A—Miss Gould brought your word."

"Miss Gould, huh," drawled Dusty. "Who was she?"

"One of us," replied the girl, darting another glance at her companions. "Did you think she was maybe a damned princess in disguise?"

"And why did Hannah send her out to do his talking?" asked Hardy.

"Figured she was smart enough to learn if we'd a chance in a fight and you wouldn't suspect her," the girl answered. "She come back, allowed there wasn't a hope and got us gals out."

"What did she tell you?" Dusty wanted to know.

"That we could come out and wouldn't be harmed and that any man who wanted was free to do the same."

"How'd Hannah take that?"

"Laughed, soldier boy, then said it'd mean a rope for any man who went out. Which it would have."

"Likely," Dusty answered.

At that moment Kiowa returned with word that he followed the woman's trail to where a horse had been hidden. She had mounted and ridden off to the north, going at a fair speed.

"You want for me to go after her, Cap'n Dusty?" the scout asked.

"How about it, Cap'n Hardy?" Dusty inquired.

"I'd say let her go. We've enough on our hands with this bunch here."

"Then how about us?" Dusty said. "Do you want my sword and guns?"

"No," Hardy replied. "Orders from Washington say that any member of your Army of Arkansas who wishes to surrender before the end of the month is free to go back to Texas with his arms."

"That's mighty obliging of your government, Captain."

"It's mighty sensible," Hardy corrected. "You darned Texans wouldn't stop fighting us any other way and we're sick of fighting you."

"In that case I'll see to burying my men, and then we'll be heading back to the regiment. We've done what we came out here for; settled Hannah's bunch for once and all."

5

THE DEATH OF
A RETIRED MAJOR

So the Civil War came to an end. True to his word, Ole Devil Hardin led his men back to Texas and dismissed them to their homes. With the end of hostilities began the task of rebuilding interrupted lives and lost fortunes.

Six years went by. Long, hard, often bitter years during which Texans worked, sweat, fought, and in some cases died to haul the Lone Star State up by its bootstraps. There was little industry in Texas and none that might compete in a national market against the more advanced techniques of the northern states. So the Texans sought for and found another means to bring money back into their impoverished land.

Not that the means took much finding, in fact it roamed almost everywhere. Through the war years, the longhorned cattle had multiplied almost unchecked across the Texas range country. When the soldiers returned, they saw a vast potential source of wealth, always assuming that they could find somebody who wished to buy their stock. When a market finally arose, the problem of delivering to it seemed at first insurmountable. The Yankee army in New Mexico and Arizona needed beef to feed various Indian tribes held on reservations. A hungry Indian never stayed long in one place and the army wanted the braves where a check could be kept upon them. Texas had the beef so badly required. All that remained was to bring produce and market together.

Like all herd-living animals, cattle could be moved on foot en masse and showed little inclination to break away from the main bunch while on the march, as long as given reasonable grazing. Bearing that fact in mind, Ole Devil Hardin, Oliver Loving, Charles Goodnight, John Chisum and other far-seeing men gathered herds and drove the assembled cattle to the army's market.

Naturally the demand of the army was limited, but the knowledge gained on those early drives paved the way to a vaster outlet for Texas's wares. Up north, in Kansas, the transcontinental railroad offered the means by which large numbers of cattle might be transported to a beef-hungry East. Using the knowledge gained on early drives, men pointed their herds north to Kansas. A long, arduous journey lay ahead; but it would be made many times.

Perhaps the Texas longhorn could not compete with Eastern beef strains in the production of succulent, tender meat, but its rivals were few, and the beef they supplied beyond the purse of the mass of people. Not so with the longhorn, despite the distance it must travel and number of intermediaries taking a cut into the profits. Its very nature fitted it for what might be termed mass production at minimal cost. At best only half-domesticated, the longhorn lived, bred, gave birth, and grew with the minimum of human supervision. A rancher need only keep a casual watch over his herd, gather such stock as he wished to market, and leave the remainder to produce a further supply.

Of course it was not always so easy. True, some men

made their fortunes, but others went broke and some died trying. For all that, by 1871 Texas stood well on its way to recovery. Reconstruction no longer reared its evil and vicious head. The corrupt and inefficient rule of Governor "Carpetbag" Davis reached its end as more and more Texans acquired sufficient wealth and power to back their demands for a voice in the state's affairs.

The years following the war had been busy and eventful for Dusty Fog. Soon after their return to the OD Connected, Ole Devil was crippled trying to ride a magnificent paint stallion. It fell on Dusty as *segundo* of the ranch to break the horse.* A matter of international importance sent him on a mission into Mexico and at its successful accomplishment he rode north. With him came two men who helped him achieve his success and who became his best, most loyal friends.† At first the trio intended to act as a floating outfit, a group of cowhands who worked the back ranges instead of being based at the ranch's main house. Due to certain prevailing conditions, they found themselves more and more sent to help people out of trouble.

Many calls for aid reached Ole Devil. In addition to the strife and hate left by war and Reconstruction, crime ran rampant through Texas. Davis's regime failed to supply any effective law enforcement. The liberal-intellectual element of it, with all the intolerance and bigotry of their kind, sought only to grind down the hated southerners who had refused to blindly conform to their beliefs, and the rest of the carpetbagger scum merely used their positions of authority as a means to line their own pockets.

So outlaw gangs roamed the state and looted practically unchecked. As always, certain names rose to prominence. James Pope Mason and Cullen Baker

* Told in *The Fastest Gun in Texas*.
† Told in *The Ysabel Kid*.

ranked high, while the Dublin brothers held Kimble County in their grip, the Marlow boys rampaged, and James Moon's sixteen-strong band operated from their hideout near Fort Ewall. Word came up of the James brothers' activities in Missouri, but Texans gave them little thought, regarding their local crop as being sufficient for their simple needs. Especially when one also included the Bad Bunch.

Nobody could say who the latter outfit might be, for a very simple reason: the Bad Bunch never left alive a witness to their crimes. Nor did they follow the patterns by which other outlaws became known, recognized, and, eventually, brought to justice. The usual run of outlaw gangs would bring off a robbery in daylight, with masked faces, drawn Colts, and escape by charging off on fast horses to the accompaniment of roaring guns. Later, after shaking off various posses that hunted them, the gang would gather in some town where the law tended to look the other way and spend much of their loot in celebration.

Not so with the Bad Bunch. Working at night, they brought off their robberies in near silence and disappeared as they came, without a trace. Posses might comb the range, led by experienced readers of sign, the Pinkerton Detective Agency send out its best men, bounty hunters scour the Texas towns and plains, or professional informers prowl alert to pick up any hint, but all to no avail. Other outlaw gangs also searched for the Bad Bunch. Some wished to merge with the efficient band that pulled such brilliant jobs. Others wished to lay hands on the Bad Bunch's stashed loot, which never came to light after once being taken.

In spite of the number of people wishing to find them, the Bad Bunch continued to strike and disappear unchecked. Now it was a bank in northeast Texas, next a bullion-loaded stagecoach, or a rancher returning from Kansas would be found dead and the proceeds of his herd's sale gone. No matter what kind of crime they committed, the Bad Bunch never left a clue.

And then the Bad Bunch made its first serious mistake. One of ignorance, maybe; unavoidable, possibly; but it brought them directly to the attention of Ole Devil Hardin.

When the Army of Arkansas disbanded, the Texas Light Cavalry split up and its members scattered over the Lone Star State. One of them was Major Beauregard Amesley. Before the war he owned and ran a successful *salle d'armes* in New Orleans. A wound in the early fighting left him with a limp incompatible with the smooth handling of a dueling sword and, anyway, the impoverished South found little need for the expensive services of a fencing master. So Major Amesley might have found himself in dire straits had Ole Devil Hardin not lent a helping hand.

As the war clouds gathered in 1860, Ole Devil gave much thought to the matter. He decided that his loyalties must lie with the South; not because he owned slaves, he did not—slavery was only one issue, though much used as a propaganda medium by the North—but through his firm belief that any sovereign state should have the right to secede from the Union if its interests clashed with the federal government. Recalling that the federal government had failed to honor its side of the bargain by which Texas had been brought into the Union—on matters such as supplying troops for defense against Indians, *comancheros* or other outlaws, to give but one example—Ole Devil elected to serve the Confederate States.

For all that Ole Devil was a realist. All too well he knew that the North possessed industry and economic power, which would be a major factor in the war. Sure the South had good fighting men; true Dixie supplied a high proportion of the U.S. Army's officers, who would return to their home states in the event of secession; but in the end the side controlling the economic situation stood the best chance. So Ole Devil made his plans. Half of his considerable fortune went to the Southern states and the remainder he banked in England. So when the war ended, Ole Devil still had money. Out in California, a gold mine supplied more. Its owner owed his success to Ole Devil's support and financial backing and honored his debt even though he wore Union blue during the war.

So Ole Devil found himself in a position to help his friends. He loaned Amesley sufficient money to start a small cutlery business, which the major made pay by producing good knives and other items of need in postwar Texas. Recently Amesley had developed a profitable sideline, instructing the families of the newly rich in Texas in the correct way to behave when in good society.

Strolling through the business section of Brownsville, his home since settling in Texas, Amesley saw a dying red glow in the waterfront district and judged that the fire must be coming under control. He wondered what had been on fire; a warehouse, from the location of the glow.

At first he thought the faint flicker of light across the street might be no more than a reflection of the distant fire. Then he realized that such could not be the case. The matter called for investigation, as the flicker showed inside the First Mercantile Bank's walls and nobody should be there at that hour of the night.

In view of the state's prevailing lawlessness, a more prudent man might have gone for help instead of crossing the street toward the bank. Amesley did not follow the prudent course. For one thing he could not be sure he saw the light and his position in town might suffer if he raised a false alarm. Also he guessed that the town's peace officers had enough on their hands at that moment. In addition to the fire, two U.S. Navy ironclads had arrived on a visit and put ashore reveling sailors who needed supervision. That threw more than sufficient work on the town's small police force without Amesley adding needlessly to it.

While crossing the street, Amesley twisted at his walking stick's handle and drew it up to make sure the sword blade concealed in the shaft moved freely. He acted in a casual manner, trying to give the impression that his change of direction had been a whim rather than caused by suspicion. Again he saw the flicker of light and guessed it showed through the glass panel in the door of the manager's office.

Although brave, Amesley was no fighting fool. He knew the limitations his lame leg placed upon him. To barge in upon the men in the office would be both stupid and suicidal. He might be a *maître d'armes* of some ability, but the sword had never been forged that could defeat a revolver across the width of a room. If he hoped to prevent a robbery, he must collect help.

Just as Amesley reached the bank's sidewalk, he heard a soft footfall. Tensing slightly, he looked in the direction of the sound and his hands gripped the sword-stick, ready to slip free the blade.

Sheriff Tim Farron, senior law-enforcement officer of Cameron County, sank exhaustedly into the chair behind his desk after spending a night watching over drunken sailors and organizing the defense against a serious warehouse fire that, if unchecked, might have destroyed half the thriving seaport city. There had been puzzling elements about that fire that he intended to investigate as soon as possible. It might have been caused by accident, but he did not rule out the chance of arson.

"Tim!" yelled the sheriff's first deputy, bursting into the office. "I just found Beau Amesley lying on the sidewalk outside the First Mercantile Bank."

"What's he doing there?" Farron growled.

"Bleeding," replied the deputy. "He's been stabbed bad and left to die."

Thrusting back his chair, Farron rose and headed for the front door. Followed by the elderly deputy, he made his way through the streets. At that early hour they had the section to themselves and, on arrival at the bank, found only the oldster's partner standing by the body. Farron looked at the bank, then down toward the still shape of an old friend. Dropping to his knees by the body, he made a careful study of it.

"Whoever killed him stood in front," Farron stated after searching the body, his voice hard and cold. "Wallet's still here and filled. Where's his stick?"

"On the road there," the younger deputy replied. "I left everything like I found it."

"Then how the—?" Farron began, but stopped and forced himself to regard the matter as a peace officer investigating a murder, not in the light of his long friendship with Amesley. His eyes went to the front of the bank. "Is everything all right in there?"

"We looked through the window and the front's all right," answered the elderly deputy. "Trouble being, the vault's in the manager's office."

"Cover Beau's face, Stet," Farron said. "Dick, you head for Banker Hoffenstall's house and ask him to come down here right away."

"Sure, Tim," replied the younger deputy. "You think—"

"I'm wanting to know, not just think about it," growled Farron.

Watching his partner turn and hurry away, Stet gave a low grunt. "What's on your mind, Tim?"

"I'm uneasy, is all," Farron replied.

Yet there was more to it than that. A shrewd, capable lawman, Farron kept in touch with other peace officers in the state. In the exchange of professional gossip had been references to a certain gang's methods of working.

Farron recalled reading of similar patterns of events to those that happened in Brownsville that night. Each time there had also been a robbery of some size.

Not that Farron wasted time in idle speculation while awaiting his deputy's return with the banker. He searched the immediate area for some clue that might lead him to Amesley's murderer, but found nothing. Nor did he find any sign of illegal entry either at the bank's main entrance or any of its other doors and windows. A feeling of helplessness filled Farron as he returned to the street. There seemed to be so little he could do to find his friend's killer—no tracks to read, no witnesses to question . . .

Once more the nagging thought returned, only more complete and clear. The pattern of the situation began to take again that definite shape. There were a number of puzzling aspects to the affair; not the least of which to Farron's way of thinking being how Amesley's killer managed to approach the major with a knife in hand. The old wound might slow Amesley's walking speed down and render him unable to indulge in fencing, but he stood firm enough on his feet. Given a level surface, like the street or sidewalk, on which to stand, Amesley should have been able to defend himself.

If the wound had been in the back, Farron could have understood it. But the striker stood in plain sight of the victim. Having considerable knowledge of knife wounds, gained during his period of office in a border town, Farron knew how and where the murderer stood to strike. From that position the knife must have been in Amesley's sight.

At that moment Dick returned with a hurrying, worried-looking Hoffenstall loping at his side. The banker looked like a prosperous undertaker, had evidently dressed in a hurry, but showed no sign of annoyance at having his sleep disturbed.

"Is he . . . ," Hoffenstall began.

"Sure is," Stet replied.

"Then who—"

"We don't now, Hans," Farron answered, knowing Hoffenstall well enough to dispense with formalities. "Done after midnight last night, or just afore it."

"And the bank?" Hoffenstall asked.

"There you've got us," admitted the sheriff. "There's no sign of anybody busting in, but I figured we'd best have you down here and take a look."

"A wise decision, Tim," said Hoffenstall, nodding approvingly. "Poor Beau. Is there nothing we can do?"

"Not a thing," Farron replied. "Let's take a look inside."

"We can't get in through the front door," Hoffenstall warned. "There are three locks on it, of which I only carry one key. My head teller and the clerk keep the others. That way no one person can enter."

"I'll send for them," Farron growled.

"I do have a key to my private office," the banker answered. "Come this way and we'll go in."

Before entering, Farron examined the lock and found no signs of tampering. Hoffenstall led the way inside and touched the lamp on his desk.

"It's still warm!" he gasped, jerking his hand away.

"Light it up and let's take a look," ordered the sheriff.

At first the lamp's light revealed nothing out of the ordinary. Then Hoffenstall reached the door of the big Chubb safe and took out his key ring. Before he selected the key, something made him try the door. A gasp of horror broke from him as it slid open.

"It . . . it's empty!" he croaked.

"Was there much in it?" asked Farron.

"Ten thousand dollars in cash and negotiable bonds, and seven thousand dollars' worth of jewelry I was holding for McKie, the ship's chandler. It's all gone. Who could have done this?"

"Offhand, I'd say there's only one outfit who could

have," Farron replied. "The Bad Bunch! Stet, go down to the Wells Fargo office and roust out their telegraph man. Send word to Ole Devil Hardin. Tell him that Beau Amesley's been murdered. I reckon he'd want to know."

6

A MIGHTY UNCONVENTIONAL LADY

The rider who brought his horse onto the trail ahead of Belle Boyd swayed in his saddle as if he either suffered from some illness or carried a fair load of Old Stump Blaster inside him. Even while Belle slowed her buggy and tried to decide which affected him, the man slid off his horse and landed limply on the ground. Bringing the buggy to a halt, Belle swung from its seat. She secured the horse to a nearby bush and glanced at the coat that lay alongside where she had sat. After another look at the man, she decided to leave the Dance Brothers Navy revolver in its holster and hidden by the jacket. Watching the man carefully, she approached him. As the girl walked up, the man gave a groan and rolled onto his back. Any doubts she might have felt died away as she saw the blood-saturated shirt and the bullet hole in his right shoulder.

Moving forward fast, Belle dropped to her knees by the man. He was young-looking, wore cowhand dress, and his face was twisted in lines of pain. As the girl came to his side, he stared around and reached weakly toward the Colt holstered at his right thigh.

"Take it easy," Belle told him, her voice a gentle southern drawl that showed culture and breeding.

"They—they're after me!" he gasped.

"Who?" she asked, studying the wound.

"Us," answered a voice from the bushes alongside the trail.

Twisting around, Belle found two men stepping into sight. Although not born or raised in Texas, she had spent enough time there to read certain signs. The newcomers might dress like cowhands, but she doubted if they earned their pay by working cattle. More likely the low-hanging gun each man wore supplied him with his livelihood. They were tall, lean men, unshaven and hard eyed; not the kind a lone girl would hope to meet on a trail far from human habitation.

For their part, the two men saw a beautiful young woman, maybe five foot eight inches in height and with a willowy build, although far from being skinny. Her face had strength of character and intelligence that did not mar its beauty. A lady's Stetson hat rode on hair so black it almost shone blue in the sun. Due to the warmth of the day, she wore no jacket. Her frilly-bosomed gray blouse, open at the throat, showed off her rich figure and ended in the waistband of a black, plain skirt, while high-heeled riding boots graced her dainty feet.

The man on the ground tried to draw his revolver, but the effort proved too much for him. With a groan, he went limp and the girl knew she could count on no help from that source.

"He's been shot," she said, coming to her feet.

"We know that," replied one of the men. "See, gal, me 'n' Dean here, we done shot him."

"Now you gone and made her all suspicious, Shem," Dean drawled, eyeing Belle in a manner likely to give a well-reared young lady an attack of the vapors.

Although Belle's upbringing had been as good as

money could buy, she failed to swoon or show any sign of fear. The men moved toward her and she stepped clear of their victim. To Dean and Shem it looked as if she backed away from them and they exchanged leers. Slowly Belle brought her hands to the waistband of her skirt and she blessed the decision to wear that particular garment while traveling.

If anybody had asked the two men what action Belle might take, they would never have guessed correctly. A tug on certain straps freed the skirt and it slid to the ground. Dean and Shem came to a halt as if they had run into a wall, and their eyes bulged out like organ stops at what they saw. Dropping the skirt, Belle revealed that she wore neither petticoats nor underskirt and went in for the latest, most daring kind of short-legged drawers. Suspender straps made black slashes over the creamy white of her thighs, and the black stockings covered legs that many a stage actress might have envied.

Neither of the men seemed able to think, which Belle counted on happening when she made the unexpected move. On other occasions when she pulled the trick, it worked equally well.

While the men remained immobile, the same did not apply to Belle. Like a flash, she glided forward a pace and whipped up her right leg to send her toe driving into Shem's groin. It was not the wild hack of a terrified girl, but the deadly attack of one well versed in the ancient French fighting art of savate. Shapely the girl's legs might be, but they packed powerful muscles as Shem discovered. A howl of pain burst from his lips and he doubled over, hands clutching at the injured area. Momentarily at least, Shem was out of the fight.

"What the he—!" Dean began, and reached toward his gun.

Swinging toward the second man, Belle shifted her weight to the rear foot, drew her left leg up and across in front of the right, and raised her body until she balanced on the ball of the right foot. Around and up whipped the left leg as she leaned her body away from Dean, delivering a wicked slashing kick to the man's face. Dean's head snapped back and his hand missed the gun's butt as he stumbled back.

From landing the *chassé croisé* kick, Belle turned and flung herself toward the buggy. Effective as savate might be as a means of self-defense, the girl knew better than to rely on it in a stand-up fight with two men; especially when she carried a more efficient answer to their menace in the buggy. Surprise gave her the chance to close fingers on the ivory grips of her Dance and she aimed to do so if she could.

Wild with rage and pain, Dean clawed out his revolver and fired. Taken in such a manner, he could not hope to achieve accuracy. For all that, the bullet hummed by Belle's head and nicked the buggy horse's ear in passing. A spirited animal, the horse reared in pain and swung around. In doing so, it collided with Belle and knocked the girl staggering. She knew that she could not halt herself and return to the buggy before Dean corrected his aim.

Even as the thought struck the girl, she became aware of the drumming of rapidly approaching hooves. Then Dean's body jerked as if struck by some unseen force and a hideous blood-spurting hole burst outward through his left cheek. His gun barked again, almost drowning the sound of a distant rifle shot, but its bullet missed the girl and he crumpled over to fall down.

During the war, and since, Belle had seen men meet violent deaths, which did not prevent her shuddering and moving her eyes hurriedly to avoid the grisly sight. Then the instinct for self-preservation caused her to act. Already Shem, holding his lower regions and showing the agony he felt, had started to draw his gun. Belle stopped staggering and flung herself toward the buggy

once more. Reaching under her jacket, she gripped and
brought into view the Dance. At the same time, she
darted a glance at the approaching rider. Although she
recognized a friend, she did not allow the knowledge to
lull her into a sense of false security. Swinging to face
Shem, she lined the Dance—a Confederate copy of the
1851 Navy Colt—and adopted the gunfighter's crouch
with practiced ease.

"Don't do it!" she warned.

Shem hesitated, his gun drawn, darting a glance toward the girl and undecided where the greater danger
lay. Tearing ever closer came a blond giant afork a
huge, but not awkward, blood bay stallion, a man fully
capable of handling any fuss that came his way. Knowing the penalty of capture, Shem elected to make a fight
for his life. He also concluded, despite the girl's capable
handling of her Dance, that the newcomer offered the
greater danger to his continued well-being.

Six foot three at least stood the newcomer, with a
great spread to his shoulders, a slim waist, and an enormous muscular development that his made-to-measure
clothes could not prevent showing. Golden blond, curly
hair showed from under his thrust-back, costly J.B. Stetson hat. An almost classically handsome face bore a
healthy, outdoor tan and showed strength. Something
of a dandy in his dress, the man gave off the unmistakable—to range-wise eyes—air of a tophand. Around his
waist hung a gun belt, matched ivory-handled Army
Colts just right for a real fast draw in the contoured
holsters.

Nor did being so large and muscular prevent him
from acting with speed. Tossing his left leg across the
saddle horn, he dropped to the ground while his big
horse still ran at speed. Shem swung toward the blond
giant, revolver slanting in the other's direction. Down
swooped the newcomer's right hand in the effortlessly
lightning-fast move that set the top-grade *pistolero*

apart from the merely good. All in one incredibly swift
action, the right-side Army Colt flowed from its holster,
cocked, and fired. Its bullet caught Shem in the chest,
spinning the man around so that his feet caught against
Dean's body. Tripping, Shem crashed to the ground,
but he felt nothing, for the blond giant's bullet had
burst through his heart.

"Howdy, Belle," the blond greeted, moving forward
cautiously to make sure Shem no longer posed any
problem. "Looks like you're in trouble, as usual."

"Only this time it's not mine," the unconventional
young lady replied, and replaced her Dance. "Did you
shoot the other one?"

"Nope. You can blame Lon for that."

Following the direction of the blond's gaze, as she
went to collect her skirt, Belle saw a second good friend
coming across the broken, bush-dotted range toward
her.

Not quite as tall as the blond, the second man also
lacked his exceptional build. Not that he gave the impression of weakness. There was a lean, whipcord
power about the man—and he looked very young. Clad
all in black, from hat clear through to boots, he had hair
the same color as Belle's. Tanned almost Indian-dark,
his handsome face gave an impression of almost babyish
innocence that did not match the wild glint in his red-
hazel eyes. Despite his apparent youth, he sat a big,
magnificent white stallion that seemed only one short
step beyond running free on the prairie, and carried
considerable armament, none of which would be for
ostentatious decoration. A walnut-handled Dragoon
Colt rode butt forward at his right side, while an ivory-
hilted James Black bowie knife hung sheathed at the
left of his belt. In his hands he gripped the Winchester
Model 1866 rifle that had saved Belle's life.

All in all, Belle once more found herself with reason
to feel pleasure at meeting Mark Counter and the

Ysabel Kid. Nor, in the latter's case, did the externals of his appearance fool her. Some folks might think of the Kid as possessing a nature in keeping with his face, but Belle was not numbered among them.

Born and raised among the Pehnane band of the Comanche Indians—his father being an Irish-Kentuckian adventurer married to the daughter of Chief Long Walker's French-Creole first wife—the Kid grew up in the manner of a young Wasp, Quick-Stinger, Raider, call them what you will, brave.* He might have turned the skills acquired during his formative years to illegal purpose had fate not brought him into contact with Dusty Fog. At that time Sam Ysabel and the Kid operated a profitable smuggling business between Texas and Mexico. Killers' lead cut down Ysabel and the Kid went after the men responsible. During the hunt he met Dusty and Mark, accepting their assistance and helping bring Dusty's mission to its successful conclusion. Finding that smuggling no longer held any attraction without his father, the Kid rode north to Texas with his new friends. From a dangerous youngster in a rough business, he developed into a useful member of range society. While not an exceptional cowhand, his talents as a scout more than made up for any deficiency. He could not claim to be fast with a handgun—although uninformed people might regard an ability to draw, shoot, and hit a man-sized target in one second fast—but considered himself adequate. Mostly at close range he made use of his bowie knife, being something of an authority with it, and set the seal against possible criticism by his unsurpassed mastery of the Winchester rifle.

That then was the Ysabel Kid. What of Belle's other rescuer?

Already Mark Counter had established a reputation for enormous strength and ability in the art of rough-

* Told in *Comanche*.

house brawling. Being something of a dandy dresser did not prevent him standing high as a working cowboy, in fact he knew few peers in that line. Third son of the owner of a large Texas ranch, rich in his own right since inheriting a maiden aunt's considerable fortune, Mark might have lived a life of leisure or owned his own spread. He much preferred to ride for the OD Connected, acting as Dusty Fog's able right bower* and being a leading member of Ole Devil's floating outfit. Although Mark's talents in some fields gained fame, his true capability with the matched Colts was not public knowledge, due to his constantly being overshadowed by the Rio Hondo gun wizard. Among the select few who knew, it was claimed that Mark ran Dusty Fog a close second in the matter of rapid withdrawal and accurate shooting.

"Howdy, Belle," greeted the Kid, dropping with cat-like grace from his stallion's low-horned, double-girthed Texas saddle. "What're they after you for this time?"

"So help me, Lon," the girl replied, donning her skirt, "I'm an innocent bystander this time."

Neither man showed any surprise at finding a well-bred southern lady acting in such an untypical manner. Of course they had the advantage of knowing Belle Boyd's story. Why the beautiful girl became one of the Confederate States' leading spies has been told elsewhere.† Along with Rose Greenhow, she became a thorn in the side of the U.S. Secret Service. That much was common knowledge. What very few people realized was that General Handiman, on taking over from Pinkerton after the war, offered Belle work in the organization she plagued so much. Always something of a tomboy, Belle accepted the offer rather than go back to her old life. The two men facing her knew of her con-

---

* Right bower: Euchre term meaning the highest trump card.
† Told in *The Colt and Sabre*.

nection with the U.S. Secret Service, having helped her on an assignment.

"This *hombre*'s hit hard," Mark commented, having crossed to and knelt by the man who started off the fuss.

"Let me see," Belle ordered, joining the blond giant.

With deft hands, she rolled open the shirt and looked down at the wound. It no longer bled, but had done so for some time. Unless Belle missed her guess, the loss of blood had caused his collapse.

"We'd best get him to town," she suggested after making her examination.

"The spread's closer," Mark answered.

"You tote him while I go fetch the doctor," the Kid drawled.

"Be best," agreed Mark. "Can I lift him, Belle?"

"Do it easy," the girl replied. "Say, how did you-all come to be on hand when I needed you?"

"Betty's on the warpath," drawled Mark with a grin.

"Which same the house's not fit for man nor beast, and we're in there someplace," the Kid went on. "So we come out looking for strays."

"We sure found them," Mark finished, and bent over the man.

Such was the blond giant's strength that he raised the unconscious man with no great difficulty and avoided opening the wound. After supervising the loading of her injured cargo, Belle climbed onto the buggy's driving seat and Mark set free her horse.

"How about those two?" she asked, indicating the bodies.

"We'll send a wagon out to collect them," Mark replied and mounted the blood bay. "Likely Hondo Fog'll know them."

"I'll tell him after I've seen the doctor," promised the Kid, swinging astride his white and starting it moving.

Between driving the buggy and watching over its passenger, Belle found little time to talk with Mark during the two-mile drive to the ranch's headquarters. Approaching the big main house, with its surrounding buildings and corrals, Belle saw General Hardin seated in his wheelchair on the porch. Time and his injury had not bowed his ramrod-straight posture, nor softened his hard fighting man's face. He wore a stylish jacket, white shirt, and string tie instead of uniform, with a blanket draped around his lower body.

At Hardin's right stood Dusty Fog. Without his uniform, he looked like a small, insignificant cowhand and contrived to make his good-quality range clothes have the appearance of somebody's castoffs.

Watching the approaching party from her place at Ole Devil's other side was a small, very beautiful girl with long black hair. Being clad in a tartan shirt, denim pants, and riding boots showed off a maturing, shapely figure, but did not distract from her air of breeding and culture. Beautiful Betty Hardin might be, yet she possessed her grandfather's temper and strength of will. Around the house nobody crossed Betty's path without regretting the act.

Dusty and Betty stepped from the porch and came toward the buggy. While the small Texan recognized Belle, he wasted no time in idle chatter. Raising his voice in a yell, he brought a couple of cowhands over from where they worked in the barn and produced the cook—by range tradition the outfit's medical adviser—out of the bunkhouse. Only when assured of help did he greet the girl who had led him through two tough assignments during the war.

"What've you been up to now, Belle?" Dusty asked.

Looking up at the skies as if seeking divine support, Belle groaned. "So help me," she said, "the next one who blames me for this—"

"Dusty!" Betty interrupted, having gone to the rear of the buggy. "This is Toby Garret, Jules Murat's *segundo*. We'd best get him into the house."

"I'll tend to it, Betty," Mark said.

"Tell Tommy to put him in the second guest room," Betty ordered as Mark gently raised the man from the bed of the buggy.

"I'll come with you, Mark," Dusty said, realizing that the wounded man might have an important message to deliver.

Watching the two men walk away, Mark carrying Garret, Betty let out an explosive snort. Then she turned to Belle and smiled.

"Since my dear cousin and his gallant friend haven't bothered, I'd better introduce myself. I'm Betty Hardin."

"I guessed," smiled Belle. "My name is Boyd—"

"Belle Boyd?" Betty said before she could stop herself.

"Disappointing, isn't it?" chuckled Belle.

"You said it, not me," Betty answered, and in that moment they became good friends. "If these two *gentlemen* will attend to your buggy, we'll go to your room."

"Betty!" barked Ole Devil, before either of the "gentlemen" could express an opinion on the matter. "I'm only the boss around here, so I suppose it's too much for me to be told what the Sam Hill's going on."

"He sounds just the same," Belle stated. "I tell you, Betty, Ole Devil was the one member of our brass in the war who almost scared me white-haired when we first met."

"He affects most folks that way, until they get to know him," Betty replied.

Recognition showed on Ole Devil's face as Belle approached. Yet, skilled as she might be, the girl read nothing on his face. Just a little nervously she held out her right hand.

"Good afternoon, General," she said. "This time I haven't come to deprive you of Dusty's services."

On both of their previous meetings Belle had been forced to ask the hard-pressed commander of the Army of Arkansas to loan her one of his best men. A twinkle flickered in Ole Devil's eyes as he studied the girl, showing the warm man under the iron-hard exterior.

"I do occasionally read my mail," he informed her. "It's a pleasure to see you again, Miss Boyd, and I hope that you enjoy your vacation with us. Wasn't that Murat's *segundo* you brought in?"

"Yes. Although I don't know either of them."

"Murat's been asked to form a Ranger company, and agreed. But I can't think what he wants here," Ole Devil remarked.

"We'll probably learn when he recovers," Betty commented. "Come on, Belle, I'll show you to your room. It'll make a change to have another girl around the house. Give me moral support, too. With the menfolks here, I need it."

7

A FACE FROM
THE PAST

While Belle willingly agreed to lend Betty the required moral support, the need for it lessened rapidly. On his arrival from Polveroso City, the doctor handed Sheriff Farron's telegraph message to Ole Devil. When he read of Amesley's murder, the rancher told Dusty, Mark, and the Kid to head for Brownsville so as to help with the investigation. A sheriff's jurisdiction ended at the boundary of his county and Farron might find the need of free agents to go out of his area, or even cross the border into Mexico, should the hunt for Amesley's killer call for such action.

Belle offered to accompany the trio in case she could help, but Dusty declined to accept. In addition to Belle's letter asking if she might spend a vacation at the OD Connected, General Handiman had also written to Ole Devil and told how the girl needed to relax after handling a dangerous assignment. Knowing that Belle had lived in deadly danger for almost three months, with death of a painful kind the penalty for a mistake, Dusty had no wish to involve her in the investigation.

He promised to send should the need arise, and Belle let the matter drop.

At dawn the trio rode out. They still did not know what brought Jules Murat's *segundo* to the OD Connected, as the man had not recovered sufficiently to talk. However, Ole Devil said they could attend to the current business. He would see to Garret and notify them if the matter be urgent.

Two days' hard riding brought Dusty, Mark, and the Kid to Brownsville. Leaving their leg-weary horses in a livery barn, they made their way to the sheriff's office and found Farron seated at his desk. He rose as the three young men entered, and greeted them warmly.

"Howdy, Dusty, boys. I hoped you'd be at the spread when my message arrived. Figured you'd be along if you were."

"Have you learned anything so far, Uncle Tim?" Dusty asked.

"Not much. But most of it points to Beau being killed by the lookout for the gang that robbed the First Mercantile Trust."

After seating his visitors, Farron went into the details. He told of the discovery of the body, the fire, and his subsequent investigations. Being a smart peace officer, Farron did not concentrate solely on trying to prove the theory he expressed to the trio. In addition, he went thoroughly into Amesley's private life in an attempt to learn of any other motive for the murder.

"I'd say Beau Amesley hadn't an enemy in the world," Dusty commented.

"And me," Farron admitted. "Can't find anybody who'd want him dead. About all I know for sure is that the warehouse fire was no accident."

"You mean somebody touched it off?" asked Mark.

"That's about the size of it," agreed the sheriff.

"Would anybody stand to gain by doing that?" asked Dusty.

"Not that I know of," Farron replied. "Way I see it, the fire was started to draw folks away from the bank."

From the way Dusty looked up and spilled tobacco out of the cigarette paper he held, Farron guessed the words meant something to the small Texan. Which figured. Dusty most likely read his father's reports on robberies in other areas.

"That's the Bad Bunch's way of working," Dusty remarked, confirming his uncle's thoughts. "I reckon Beau must've come on them while they were in the bank. But that'd be late on, I'd reckon. Where'd Beau been?"

"Down at the Barrelhouse Theater most of the evening, but I don't know after that," Farron answered. "Maybe you could learn."

"We'll make a whirl at it," Dusty promised. "The thing I don't see is the lookout walking up to Beau Amesley and using the knife without getting a gut full of cold steel."

"Didn't Beau have his sword-stick along?" Mark went on, for Farron had mentioned that Amesley was stabbed from the front.

"It was lying close to him, unscrewed but not pulled."

"The feller could have throwed the knife in," the Kid said.

"It's been pushed in and ripped across," stated Farron. "And by a real top hand, or I've never seen one's work."

"Anybody in town'd fit?" Dusty asked.

"We're long on good knife men down here," Farron told him. "Only I don't see any of them working with the Bad Bunch."

"Whoever it was, he'd have to be *real* good to drop Beau Amesley," the Kid asserted. "I tell you, I wouldn't've liked to try it."

"You got any ideas, Lon?" Dusty demanded.

"Nope. But unless the law's got 'round to stringing ole Cisco Castro up, he might have some."

"We haven't," the sheriff said, sounding sightly rueful at having failed to bring off the "stringing up."

"Reckon I'll go see him tonight," drawled the Kid.

"You needing help?" Dusty inquired.

"Be best if I went alone," the Kid replied, and his friends yielded to superior knowledge.

"Mind if we ask questions, Uncle Tim?" Dusty said.

"That's why I asked you to come," Farron replied. "You're seeing things from the outside, not up close like me. I'll deputize you if you like."

"It'll be best," Dusty agreed. "But we'll keep the badges hidden for a spell."

"Play it any way you want," confirmed the sheriff.

"I'll try to see the banker tonight," Dusty said. "Mark, you take the theater. I want to know where Beau went after he left. I'll leave you to handle your end, Lon."

During the time circumstances forced them to wear law badges in a tough Montana gold town,* the trio had handled two murder investigations. So they knew the routine and could be relied upon to delve deeper than Farron felt he might when dealing with personal friends. After being officially deputized, although they did not wear their badges, the trio left the sheriff's office. Watching them go, Farron let out a long sigh.

"Lord help you, whoever you are, if those three lay hands on you," he said.

On giving the matter some thought, Dusty called off his visit to the bank until the following morning. Already the sun sank in the west and he did not wish to present himself in Hoffenstall's office with the marks of two hard days' riding on him. From what he knew of bankers in general, Dusty realized that his first impression must be right if he hoped to gain the other's confi-

* Told in *Quiet Town*.

dence. So he decided to leave the meeting until more suitably attired. Mark agreed with the suggestion and the Kid also wished to change clothes before making his foray into the cantina of Cisco Castro.

So the trio collected their war bags from the livery barn and went to Farron's house. The sheriff had already warned his wife and she insisted that the cowhands roomed there instead of at a hotel. With their accommodation settled, Dusty, Mark and the Kid made their preparations for the evening.

At half past eight, bathed and dressed in clean clothing, Dusty and Mark drifted into the Barrelhouse Theater. So far the eastern trend of placing the audience in neat rows of seats had not found favor in Texas. Customers sat at tables, lounged along the bar, or wandered up and down the room, drinking, sampling the lavish freelunch counter's offerings, and enjoying the entertainment.

Although sparse at that early hour, the audience gave rowdy support to a pair of knockabout comics on the stage. With an experienced eye, one of the waiters studied the new arrivals. He made a rapid, and accurate, estimation of the cost of their clothes. Deciding that both were used to dressing well and not merely fancied up for a visit to a big town, he headed in their direction.

"A table, gents?" he asked with the air of conferring a favor on them.

"Why, sure," Mark replied.

"Over here do?" asked the waiter, indicating a table with a good view of the stage. Then he nodded meaningfully to a number of flashily dressed young women scattered about the room. "Would there be anything else?"

"Sure," agreed Dusty.

"Which two?" inquired the waiter.

"Which was Beau Amesley with on Tuesday?" Dusty asked.

A furtive glint came to the waiter's eyes and confirmed certain conclusions Dusty had formed on the affair. From the start Dusty guessed that the reticence concerning Amesley's movements stemmed from a woman being involved. It seemed that stringent orders had been given concerning the matter, for the waiter gulped and threw a scared look around him.

"I don't know what you mean." He gulped and began to move away.

"Hold it, *hombre!*" ordered Mark, dropping a big hand on to the waiter's shoulder. "We want to know the answers."

For a moment the waiter thought of raising a fuss, but changed his mind as he felt the power in the blond giant's fingers. None of the theater's bouncers had made their appearance so far, and even if any should be present, those two cowhands looked tough enough to make things mighty painful for the waiter before the man made any decision.

"Hey there," said a woman's voice from behind the Texans. "Put him down, handsome. It's too early in the evening for that kind of thing."

Turning, Dusty and Mark studied the speaker. She proved to be a middle-sized woman in her late thirties, with a plump, rubbery build. Although stage makeup covered her face and she wore her blond hair piled up in the latest theatrical fashion, Dusty felt sure he knew her. Clad in a more expensive version of the clothes worn by the other female occupants of the room, she clearly did not follow their profession and the waiter showed obvious relief at seeing her.

Maybe Dusty would not have been so positive in his identification if he had not recently been in Belle Boyd's presence. As it was, he recognized the woman. The voice, with its English accent, helped.

"You're a long way from New Orleans, English Flo," he said.

Surprise, mingled with not a little worry, came to the woman's face. She stared long and hard at Dusty before recognition flickered into her eyes.

"You!" she gasped.

"Me," admitted Dusty. "I was asking this jasper about Beau Amesley."

"Let him go and tend to his work," the woman requested. "I can tell you all you need to know. And I don't know who you thought I was, but I'm Madam Flora, and this is my place."

"My mistake, ma'am," Dusty replied, and nodded to Mark, who released the waiter. "You'll be the one we want to see anyways."

After the waiter departed, Madam Flora waved the Texans into chairs at a secluded table. Worry flickered on the woman's face as she looked at Dusty.

"All right," she said. "What do you want to know?"

"Where Beau Amesley went after he left here," the small Texan replied. "And who he went with."

"What's it mean to you?"

"Plenty. He was a good friend in the war, and the things he taught me about handling a sword saved my life more than once. So I aim to get his killer."

"I never did learn your name," Madam Flora remarked, "or the girl's, come to that."

"She was Belle Boyd," Dusty replied. "And I'm Dusty Fog."

"Belle Boyd, huh?" repeated Madam Flora thoughtfully. "I could have beaten her if she hadn't started kicking."

"Likely that's why she started," Dusty grinned.

On his second mission with Belle Boyd, Dusty penetrated Union territory to the city of New Orleans. Needing the help of an expert safe blower, they visited the saloon of a notorious gang boss. The price he placed on his assistance had been that Belle fought with Madam Flora—English Flo as she had been then—in a bare-knuckle boxing match.* Despite Dusty's objections, Belle agreed and used her knowledge of savate to offset the other woman's extra weight and greater experience.

Having been in Belle's presence a short time before helped Dusty identify Madam Flora, and he could understand the blond's desire not to have her past brought into the open. It seemed that she threw off her old New Orleans associates and ran a profitable, legitimate business, which might be adversely affected if word of her past leaked out.

While Dusty did not intend to do the leaking, he figured Madam Flora would be mighty cooperative as long as she felt he might.

"Beau left here alone," Madam Flora stated after the waiter brought drinks.

"At what time?" asked Mark.

"Around midnight."

"That's not what you told Tim Farron," Dusty reminded her.

More worry lines creased the woman's face and she glanced around to make sure that nobody other than the Texans might hear her. Even after taking the precaution she dropped her voice to almost a whisper.

"Look, Cap'n Fog. There're some mighty important names mixed in this—"

"That figures. And I still want to know."

"It could cost me this place."

"So could folks learning that you're English Flo," Dusty pointed out.

Inadvertently he had struck harder than he realized. At a party in a U.S. Navy officers' club on a New Orleans shore base, while celebrating the end of the war, English Flo had been persuaded to fight one of the women guests. Everybody being drunk, little damage ought to

* Told in *The Rebel Spy*.

have been done. However, the other woman, daughter of a prominent Radical Republican politician, fell awkwardly, struck her temple against a table's edge, and died. A warrant was sworn out for Flo's arrest, but she fled. Knowing her fate if caught, she made for Texas. Hard work had put her in charge of the Barrelhouse Theater and nobody now connected Madam Flora with English Flo, wanted murderess and associate of some of the worst thieves ever to plague New Orleans.

"You don't give me much choice," Madam Flora groaned.

"Beau Amesley didn't have any choice, either," Dusty growled. "Look, ma'am, I won't say who you are whether you help me or not. But I aim to get Beau's killer and you can help me."

"It's likely that the fellers he was with don't know a thing about him getting killed," Mark went on. "But we have to know."

"And any name you mention's safe with us," Dusty promised. "They'll not know who told us."

Watching the two men, Madam Flora found herself believing them. "All right, then," she said. "The Uptown Fishing, Hunting, and Inside-Straight Club held a private party in a suite upstairs."

"Who are they?" asked Dusty.

"Like I said, prominent men. Sportsmen who go hunting and fishing together."

"Names," Dusty said.

"Beau was one. There's McKie, the chandler. Colonel Mayne, the lawyer. Judge Noire, Banker Hoffenstall, about a dozen of them."

As Flora rattled off the names, Dusty could see why Farron did not push the investigation any further. The smooth running of his office depended on his relations with most of the men mentioned. Not that it would have stopped Farron if he thought the killing tied in with the club. As it apparently did not, the sheriff pre-

ferred Dusty to handle that end of the affair; to act as a
whipping boy in case of objections. Backed by the
power of Ole Devil Hardin's name and his own reputation, Dusty fitted ideally into the sheriff's needs.

"What kind of a party?" the small Texan asked.

"They had some drinks—and a few of the girls went
up there. Which same all but Beau were married."

"Gals?"

"Don't act coy, Cap'n!" Flora snorted. "The gals
aren't around just to enjoy the show. The club had five
or six of them in the room for supper and to play poker."

"Which girls went?"

"So help me, Captain, I don't know. They come from
Mama Lola's place down on Conception. She might
know."

"We'll ask her, then," Dusty said. "That way nobody'll
bring it back to you."

"Thanks," Flora breathed. "Do you know where Conception Street is?"

"I've got a right good guide here," Dusty replied,
nodding to Mark.

"For shame, Dusty," drawled the blond giant. "You'll
ruin my good name."

Like the theater, Mama Lola's house had not begun
its evening's main business when the two Texans arrived. A couple of girls stood talking at one side of the
lounge, while a pair of brawny bouncers sat idly playing
cards with a tall, slim young man clad in a fancy city
suit. Beaming delightedly, Mama Lola advanced on the
Texans with her usual friendly welcome. It did not stay
friendly for long when she heard what brought them to
her establishment.

"I don't know what you mean," she said sullenly. "If
you want gals, I got 'em. If you want to ask questions, go
find a priest."

"Don't fuss us, Mama," Mark warned. "We aim to see
the—"

A snap of Mama's fingers brought the two bouncers to their feet and they approached the Texans from the rear. Unfortunately for him, the man behind Dusty arrived first. Reaching out his big left hand, the bouncer caught Dusty's right forearm, ready to pull the small Texan around and fell him with a right fist's punch. Only things did not go as planned.

Showing the same devastating speed as when drawing a gun, Dusty's left hand flashed across to catch the bouncer's left wrist. At the same moment, the small Texan slid free his gripped arm and entwined it around the man's at the bicep. Moving at a speed that left the other no chance to object, Dusty pivoted his body and dragged the trapped arm to the left. Bowing his knees sightly, Dusty drove his right leg back against the bouncer's to further throw the man off balance. So swiftly and effectively did the small Texan move that the bouncer went over his right hip and flew across the room to land hard on the floor.

Taken by surprise, the second bouncer paused and stared. Mark came around in a fast turn, his right hand clamping hold of the man's throat. Then the blond giant gave a surging heave and flung the bouncer away. Staggering and turning, the man smashed into the wall face first and slid downward with a moan.

The sound of a chair scraping back drew Dusty's eyes to the table vacated by the bouncers. He saw a well-dressed man starting to rise and reaching under the city jacket. With the same speed used when throwing the bouncer, Dusty sent his right hand to the butt of the left-side Colt. Half a second later, the slim man stared into the .44 bore of the white-handled revolver.

"Sit down!" Dusty ordered. "If there's one thing I hate, it's a mac."

Although the slim man might have wished to object to being called a "mac", knowing it to be the Texans' name for a pimp, he wisely said nothing. Such incredible speed with a gun was almost invariably accompanied by sufficient accuracy to place a bullet into a man-sized target at close range.

"Don't shoot him!" Mama yelled, while the man flopped back into his chair and kept empty hands in plain view.

"Then you start talking, and don't lie," Dusty answered.

"What do you want to know?" she moaned.

"Which of your girls went to the party upstairs at the theater on the night Beau Amesley died."

"Who told you about that?"

"One of my spread's cowhands was in and he 'heard talk,'" Dusty lied, holstering his Colt and watching his victim crawl painfully erect.

"There were six of 'em," Mama said as the bouncer limped out of the room.

"Which six?" asked Mark. "We want to talk to them."

"I've only got five of them here now," Mama replied worriedly.

"Where's the other?" Dusty snapped.

"She pulled out yesterday. Wasn't here more than two weeks."

"Where'd she go?"

"Damned if I know," Mama answered bitterly. "She's not in town, that's for sure. Or if she is, somebody'll regret stealing her from me."

"Was she something special?" Dusty inquired.

"Hell yes," Mama replied. "A real beauty. Why, Banker Hoffenstall used to ask for her all the time."

"He did, huh?" Dusty said.

"Sure. A gal like her's worth money. If she's around town and working for some other house, I'll . . ."

Mama allowed her words to trail away, suddenly realizing that she had said more than she ought. Guessing they would learn no more from the old woman, Dusty told her he wanted to question the remaining girls.

Grudgingly Mama gave permission and requested the Texans did their questioning in her private room. Although Dusty and Mark questioned each girl, they learned nothing to point to Amesley's murder being connected with the other members of the party. Nor did they gain much information about the sixth girl, for she had never mixed with her fellow workers except in business hours and did not talk about her past.

FLINT
IF HE HAD TO DIE, AT LEAST IT WOULD BE ON HIS TERMS..

Get a taste of the *true* West, beginning with the tale of *FLINT* FREE for 15 Days

Hunted by a relentless hired gun in the lava fields of New Mexico, Flint "*settled down to a duel of wits that might last for weeks...Surprisingly, he found himself filled with zest for the coming trial...So began the strange duel that was to end in the death of one man, perhaps two.*"

If gripping frontier adventures capture your imagination, welcome to The Louis L'Amour Collection! It's a handsome, hardcover series of thrilling sagas by the world's foremost Western authority and author.

Each novel in The Collection is a true-to-life portrait of the Old West, depicted with gritty realism and striking detail. Each is enduringly bound in rich, Sierra-brown leatherette, with padded covers and gold-embossed titles. And each may be examined and enjoyed for 15 days. FREE. You are never under any obligation; so mail the card at right today.

Now in handsome Heritage Editions

Each matching 6" x 9" volume in The Collection is bound in rich Sierra-brown leatherette, with padded covers and embossed gold title... creating an enduring family library of distinction.

SILVER CANYON·LOUIS L'AMOUR
THE DAYBREAKERS·LOUIS L'AMOUR
FLINT·LOUIS L'AMOUR

8

THE KID ACQUIRES NEGATIVE INFORMATION

While Dusty and Mark could hardly be said to move in the cream of Brownsville's society, the Ysabel Kid most definitely passed through the town's lowest social level. True, there were honest, hardworking Mexicans living in that area, but not in the section where the Kid walked. He moved cautiously, prowling along with all the wary alertness of a hunting cougar, knowing that men had been murdered in the Mexican quarter for far less than a Dragoon Colt and a James Black bowie knife. Ahead stood the well-lit, substantial shape of Cisco Castro's cantina, the most prosperous—and dangerous—place in the district. Brave man though he might be, Tim Farron would not have passed through the streets and visited Castro's place at night unless backed by at least two deputies armed with shotguns. The cantina catered to some of the worst scum of the border and seacoast, in addition to various range-bred cutthroats. Yet the Kid went there alone.

Where his two friends tidied up their appearance, the Kid made no attempt to do so. He changed his clothing, donning a blue shirt, denim pants and gaudy bandanna,

all of which showed signs of hard use and had been
brought along on the chance that he might need them.
Dressed that way, his face unshaven since leaving the
OD Connected, the Kid no longer looked young or
innocent. While he retained his gun belt and armament, he felt satisfied with his disguise as he approached one of the most dangerous tasks in an eventful
young life.

Although several years had elapsed since his last visit,
the Kid found the cantina little changed. Much the
same kind of men loafed about the room, evil faced and
hard eyed; Mexican and American criminals of the
worst kind, existing in amity brought about by a mutual
need for protection against a hostile world. Pretty girls
in garish dresses moved about the room, entertaining
the customers and serving out drinks. They, like the
men, studied the newcomer; although the girls showed
more interest and less hostility.

Standing behind the bar, Cisco Castro examined the
Kid with puzzled eyes. He felt that he ought to know
the newcomer, yet could not place the face. A small,
slender man, with a hooked nose and bearded face,
Castro managed to give the impression of benevolence
and was about as evil as any one man could manage.

"Hey, handsome," greeted a girl as the Kid reached
the bar. "You buy me a drink, maybe?"

"Give her one, friend," requested the Kid. "Then tell
her to *vamos* while me'n'you make talk."

"You don't like Maria, maybe, *señor?*" Castro asked.

"She'd do fine—happen that's what I'd come here
after."

"Then what do you want?" the cantina owner said,
motioning the girl to go away.

"I want to change some money," the Kid replied, and
drew a new hundred dollar bill from his pocket, placing
it on the bar top.

"Just that?" Castro inquired.

"It's got friends. Eight thousand dollars worth of 'em."

"Here?"

"Outside town with my four pards. You don't reckon I'd be hawg-stupid enough to bring it down here with me, now do you?"

"You don't trust me, *señor?*" purred Castro.

"Now why'd you-all go thinking a fool thing like that?" drawled the Kid. "Only there's some mighty dishonest folks around and I didn't want to get my pocket picked coming here."

Apparently the explanation satisfied Castro. A grin came to his face and he jerked his head toward the center of three doors leading from the main barroom. "Come with me, *señor.*"

Conscious of watching eyes, the Kid joined Castro at the end of the counter and accompanied him to the indicated door. A couple of Mexicans rose in a deliberately casual manner and slouched across the room toward the right-side door.

"Tell them to go back and sit a spell," ordered the Kid.

"Who, *señor?*" asked Castro mildly.

"Those two jaspers you wigwagged to as you come along the bar."

"You have sharp eyes, my friend," Castro smiled and signaled to the men who returned to their seats. "After you."

The last words came as the cantina owner thrust open the center door and waved a hand to it. However, the Kid did not intend to be outdone in the matter of politeness and insisted that Castro lead the way. Giving a shrug, the man entered first and the Kid followed with caution, which proved to be needless.

Luxurious was the only way to describe Castro's private office. Thick carpets covered the floor, paintings hung on the walls, the desk might have graced an old southern mansion, and a Chubb safe stood in one corner. At the right of the room, heavy drapes hung before an alcove leading to Castro's living quarters.

Taking a seat at his desk, Castro offered the Kid first a cigar, then tobacco when the other expressed an intention of rolling his own smoke. Again the Kid declined and Castro shrugged calmly, requesting that they commence their business.

"Like I said. Me'n'the boys have this money to change. All in new bills, which same we can't spend without bringing the Pinkertons down on us."

"And may I ask where the money came from?" Castro said. "Come now, I must know the risks involved before quoting a price. I doubt if you expect them changed at a dollar for a dollar."

"We hit the bank at Tascosa," the Kid answered.

"Tascosa, you say," repeated Castro. "That is strange. I have not heard of such a piece of business."

"They do say you know plenty that goes on," admitted the Kid. "It's even said you know who sold Juarez's brother to the French."

For a moment the smile left Castro's face and recognition flared on it. His hands slapped on the desktop in what appeared to be a nervous gesture. Only the Kid knew different.

Moving with the speed of his Comanche forefathers, the Kid turned toward the drapes. His fingers closed around the butt of the bowie knife, sliding it from its sheath. While the bowie knife could best be thrown by gripping the blade, its superb design and balance also allowed it to work when held by the handle. So the Kid did not need to take the split second necessary to make the change of hold. Up and down swung his arm and the room's lamps glinted on flying steel as the knife hissed through the air. Eleven and a half inches of razor-edged steel converged with the man who burst through the drapes. Its point pierced the man's flesh just under the center of his ribs, while the concave and convex curves of the blade combined to open a passage and allow entrance to the two-and-a-half-inch width. Sinking home almost hilt deep, the knife doubled its victim over, stifled all but a croaking gasp of pain, and tumbled him helplessly down.

Without even pausing to see the result of his throw, the Kid kept his hand moving. Turning palm outward, it gripped and drew the Dragoon to line the barrel on Castro.

"You should ought to try something new, Castro," said the Kid. "Set and keep your hands where I can see them."

Having relied upon his hidden man to take care of the Kid, Castro failed to make a move until too late. The other pair of men had been a decoy, holding the visitor's attention while a third entered Castro's living quarters and hid behind the drapes in case he should be needed. Such a trick had worked well on other occasions, so Castro did not feel the need to take a hand. When he realized that his plan failed, the cantina owner found himself looking into the two-inch-wide bore—or so it seemed when seen from that angle—of the Kid's Dragoon Colt. Obediently Castro remained in his seat and placed his hands palm down on the desktop.

"Who are you?" he hissed.

"You'd know me as Cabrito," the Kid replied.

"Cabrito!" breathed Castro, showing that the old magic still held in the Kid's border name. "Then it was a trick."

"Why, sure," agreed the Kid cheerfully. "Ole Mark had that new hundred on him and I knew you'd fetch me in here to talk about it. You never do business out in front of that bunch."

"What do you want, Cabrito?" asked Castro bitterly.

"Names, Cisco."

"And if I don't give them?"

"I send word to Juarez."

"You have no proof."

A mocking smile twisted the Kid's lips and did not reach his eyes. "Are you game to bet on it?"

Clearly Castro was not. Sweat stood out on his forehead and he ran his tongue tip across dry lips. All too well he knew what his fate would be if Benito Juarez suspected his part in the incident mentioned by the Kid. Being *presidente* of Mexico would not stop Juarez seeking revenge and, in fact, gave him a greater chance of arranging it.

"What names?" Castro snarled.

"I want to know who the Bad Bunch are," replied the Kid.

Worry creased Castro's face. "I don't know. *Madre de Dios,* Cabrito, that is the truth."

"Don't fuss me none, Castro!" spat the Kid. "You know every damned outlaw from here to the Indian nations and back the long way."

"Not the Bad Bunch, Cabrito," stated Castro, with such fervor that the Kid felt inclined to believe him.

Not that the Kid allowed any hint of his belief to show. "You wouldn't be lying to an old friend, Cisco. Now would you?"

"I'm not, Cabrito. This is the truth. I've no idea who they are; and I've tried to find out."

That figured to anybody who knew Castro. If any man in Texas knew the identity of the Bad Bunch, other than its members, the Kid would have bet on Castro being the one. With an eye on profit from the gang's efforts, Castro was sure to have tried to learn their identity. Clearly he did not succeed. Fear of Juarez's vengeance would have made him amenable to the Kid's wishes.

Realizing that he could learn no more, the Kid gave thought to taking his departure. Happen he hoped to reach the safe part of town, he must handle things real careful. With that thought in mind, he prepared to retrieve his weapon.

A glance told him that he need not fear any action from the stricken man. Moving carefully, the Kid edged across the room and bent down to pluck the knife from the body of Castro's bodyguard. At no time while collecting the knife and wiping its blade clean on the body's clothes did the Kid take his Dragoon out of alignment with Castro, or offer the cantina owner a chance to make a hostile move.

"Who-all's the second best knife fighter in town, Cisco?" he asked, sliding the bowie into its sheath.

"Second best. . . ."

"I'm here for the first best," drawled the Kid modestly.

"There are several good knife men," Castro pointed out.

"And you know 'em all," the Kid answered. "Was one of them hired to kill Beau Amesley?"

"How would I know—" Castro began.

"You'd know, Cisco. There's not a move made in this town you don't know about. Was there?"

"If there was, I didn't hear of it."

Watching Castro's face, the Kid once more felt the other spoke truthfully. A man with sufficient skill to kill Amesley in such a manner would be hard to find. If such a man came from Brownsville, Castro was sure to know him. Which meant that the Bad Bunch had along a mighty skilled hand with a fighting knife; and one whose name was not yet known—or not suspected—as a member of the mysterious gang.

"Name me some names," the Kid ordered.

"The two best are Ortiz and Diego, but they—"

"Go on," encouraged the Kid, and made a gesture with his Colt.

"On Tuesday night neither were in Brownsville," Castro continued, knowing better than try the Kid's patience too far. "I sent—they went into Mexico on business last week and have not returned yet."

"Any more?"

"Look, Cabrito, I know how Amesley died. I also know how he could use that sword-stick he carried. Whoever killed him was good, very good. In fact I don't believe either Ortiz or Diego even would have been good enough. Yet they, with apologies to you, are the best I know."

"You tried to learn his name, the bastard who killed Beau Amesley?"

"Of course."

That figured. Always in the market for superior talent, being an agent for the hiring of professional killers among his other sins, Castro could be expected to make inquiries. Yet the Kid felt sure Castro spoke the truth when mentioning the matter. No man of Castro's reputation cared to admit failure and he could not hold down a bitter note as he said the two words. Despite his organization for gathering information, he had failed to learn the identity of the Bad Bunch or locate the expert knife-handler who ended Amesley's life.

"You didn't get his name, then?" said the Kid, more as a statement than in a question.

"No!" spat Castro.

"You've not helped me much at all," the Kid said. "Reckon I'll be going, Cisco. I'll use the back way."

"There's no door. . . ."

A cold, mocking gleam flickered in the Kid's eyes and his lips drew back with the mocking grin of a coup-hunting Comanche dog soldier. "You wouldn't be trying to rile me, now would you, Cisco?"

Perhaps the only good thing one could credit to Castro was his courage. He might be as morally evil as humanly possible, yet cowardice could not be claimed among his vices. For all that he felt an icy hand run over him as he watched the Kid's expression. At that moment Castro stood very close to death and he knew it. He also realized that the Kid remembered the layout of the building and so did not continue with the bluff.

"Use the door in my room," Castro offered.

"Come and open it for me," suggested the Kid.

Obediently, for the Kid left him no choice of being otherwise, Castro left his seat and led the way into his private quarters. While the office did not offer a rear exit, the second room did. Unlocking and opening the door, Castro stood aside to let the Kid leave.

"Happen you learn anything, Cisco," the Kid said, "send me word."

"I will remember," Castro replied. *"Hasta la vista,* Cabrito."

"You don't mean that, I'll bet," said the Kid, and faded off into the darkness.

Fury twisted Castro's face as he slammed the door and locked it. If the Kid had not passed his information to Juarez, it seemed unlikely he would do so now. Certainly not as a means of blind revenge. Yet only two people alive knew that Castro betrayed and sold Juarez's brother to the French during the struggle to obtain Mexican freedom from foreign rule, everyone else involved having died mysteriously. Two, in Castro's opinion, was one too many. It mattered little where the Kid learned the guilty secret. Castro could never rest easy with the young Texan possessing such knowledge.

Which brought up a tricky point; who could remove the Kid's menace to Castro's well-being? Not a regular member of the cantina owner's staff. Knowing the close ties that bound the floating outfit and the loyalty of the remainder of the OD Connected crew, Castro did not intend to bring them down on his head. So he must cover his tracks and use men with no direct connection to his band.

With that thought in mind, Castro returned to the barroom and looked about him in search of likely candidates. He gave no thought to the dead bodyguard, beyond annoyance at the mess on his fine carpeting, and located the men he needed. There would be time after dispatching the men to have the body removed. Crossing the room, Castro signaled to the required men and they obediently left the room. A short time later, Castro followed them.

Despite having made such an easy and peaceful exit from the cantina, the Kid remained vigilant as he passed through the streets. Nor did he relax to any great extent when beyond the Mexican quarter and heading toward the sheriff's home. Walking along, he listened to the night noises and cursed the ever-present sounds of the town. Out on the open range a man might safely rely upon his ears, but not so in a big town with its clamor of continuous din.

Strolling through a section given over to business premises connected with the port, and deserted at that time, the Kid directed his feet toward the sheriff's home, where he could change before joining his friends.

Almost too late his ears caught the unmistakable hiss of a well-thrown knife as it rushed through the air in his direction from an alley across the street. No white man could have escaped injury, but the Kid moved with all the speed of a Pehnane brave-heart. For all that, as he dropped toward the ground with his right hand fanning to the hilt of his knife, he felt the wind of his enemy's missile as it brushed by the back of his shirt. A yell, like a man in mortal pain, broke from the Kid and masked without drowning out entirely the thud as the knife sank into the wall beyond him.

To the watching pair of men it both looked and sounded as if the first's knife struck home. So they rushed forward without exercising any great caution, wanting to lay hands on the loot promised by Castro. Ahead of his pard, the knife's thrower bent forward and reached out a hand toward the shape that lay on its back before him. Suddenly the victim's left hand shot up, gripped the man's wrist, and heaved hard. Taken by surprise and off balance, the man shot forward, tripped over the Kid's body, and fell straight onto the bowie knife as it lashed to meet him. With a surging heave, the Kid tore open the man's belly. Spewing out entrails, the would-be killer continued forward, smashed into the nearby wall, and went down.

Seeing his partner's fate, the second man skidded to a turn and tried to escape. The Kid rolled over on the ground, stabbing out his free hand to catch the man's ankle and heave. As the other crashed down, the Kid lunged forward and rammed a knee into the center of his back. Digging fingers into the man's lank, greasy hair, the Kid dragged his head back and placed the bowie's blade in position to cut his throat.

"Who are you?" growled the Kid.

"Juan Moreno, *señor*," whined the man, noting the faultless border-Spanish spoken by his captor.

"You're not one of Castro's regular bunch," growled the Kid. "Did he tell you my name?"

"Only that you had much money, which he said we could keep half of if we found and killed you."

"Go back and tell him that you failed. I thought he hadn't told you my name. A *pelado** like you wouldn't dare go up against El Cabrito if you knew."

"You are El Cabrito?" gasped the man.

"That's me," agreed the Kid, moving back and letting the man rise. "I didn't reckon you knew. It'd've riled me if you had. I wouldn't want to think Castro rated me so low he reckoned only two, and a pair like you, could take me. *Vamos, pronto!*"

Being well aware of the reputation built by the Kid during his smuggling years, the man raised no objec-

---

* Pelado: Thief of the lowest kind, a corpse robber.

tions and scuttled away like a rabbit hunting cover. Nor did he stop until he reached Castro's place with word of the Kid's escape. For that he received a knife in the belly from a furious, and scared, cantina owner.

Looking down at the body, Castro knew his time in Texas had come to an end. Maybe the treacherous attack would bring the Kid back with reinforcements; or he might even pass on his knowledge to Juarez. In either case Castro's life expectancy could be mighty limited. Flight was the answer, but he must decide correctly where to go. Should Juarez learn the truth, Mexico, or anywhere near it, would be a mighty unhealthy location. Turning over various possibilities, Castro decided that Cuba offered a man of his talents the greatest opportunities, being well removed from Mexico, inadequately policed and ruled, and offering a land where his native tongue was spoken. He concluded there had best be no delay in arranging his passage and sent a trusted man to learn if any boat in the harbor headed for Cuba in the next few days.

Unaware of the service he had rendered to Brownsville, the Kid continued his interrupted walk toward the sheriff's house. He realized that he possessed only negative information. But that could often prove of use.

9

THE POWER OF OLE DEVIL'S NAME

"Come in, Captain Fog," Hoffenstall greeted, standing behind his Negro maid and beaming at the small Texan.

"I reckon this's hardly the time to call and talk business, Mr. Hoffenstall," Dusty said, entering the house and handing his hat to the maid. "Trouble being that I only just pulled in and have to leave as soon as I'm sure Beau Amesley's company's in good hands."

"Of course. I understand. If you will come into my study . . ."

In view of the information gained at Mama Lola's house, Dusty once more revised his decision about visiting the banker. He wanted to strike before any word could reach Hoffenstall. Maybe Mama Lola, wishing to curry favor or clear herself of blame, would notify the banker of Dusty's visit and what the small Texan had learned. If that happened, Dusty was unlikely to gain any information from the banker.

Relying on the power of Ole Devil's name, Dusty told Mark and Farron of his intentions. Despite their acceptance of the Kid's plan, neither Dusty nor Mark felt happy about their *amigo* going alone to Castro's place.

So Mark said he would wait at Farron's home in case the
Kid needed help on returning from the Mexican quarter.

Taking Dusty into his study, Hoffenstall seated him in
a comfortable chair and offered the customary courtesies. With a glass of imported brandy in one hand and an
expensive cigar glowing in the other, Dusty got down to
business.

"I reckon you know that my uncle's a major shareholder in Beau's company?"

"I'd say partner, to be more accurate," Hoffenstall
answered.

"Call it what you want. General Hardin sent me
down to arrange for somebody to run things at this end.
He can't get here and wants a good man in charge until
Beau's affairs're straightened out."

"My bank's facilities are at your service, Captain
Fog."

"I heard that you had a robbery."

"Yes," admitted Hoffenstall. "But I assure you that the
loss was not great and we are entirely sound."

"Sound financially, maybe," Dusty drawled. "But are
you safe?"

"I don't follow you," Hoffenstall said, looking as if he
wanted to ask for his drink and cigar back.

"You know Tim Farron's my uncle, I reckon?"

"Yes."

"Well, he told me about the holdup. Seems like that
bunch got into the bank and opened its safe without
raising sweat, noise, or fuss. I don't know what Uncle
Tim thinks, but it looks an inside job to me."

"An inside job?" squawked Hoffenstall. "Do you realize what you're saying?"

"I'm only saying what you must've been thinking all
along."

"And I assure you, Captain Fog, that I've never regarded there being any possibility of an inside job as you call it."

"Show me I'm wrong. Uncle Devil was mighty concerned about leaving Beau's money in a bank that gets robbed so easily."

"The bank itself did not get robbed. I doubt if any gang could have broken into our main vault with such ease."

"You can convince me of that?"

"I can allow you to inspect the premises and make your own decision," Hoffenstall snorted. "Not tonight, but in the morning if you wish. In fact I could do it tonight if I send for two of my men."

With that, Hoffenstall explained his security arrangements and Dusty listened carefully. At last the small Texan nodded.

"It all sounds safe enough," Dusty stated. "But the gang still got in."

"To my private office, that's all," corrected Hoffenstall. "Each night before we leave, I check every door and window is secure. Then we bolt the connecting door to my office from the bank's side. Leave by the front door and all three of us lock it. After that I go around to my office, enter, bolt the connecting door on my side, and lock the other door on my way out. The vault has the latest in locks and its door is in plain view of the windows, with a lantern left burning so as to illuminate it."

"That's safe enough. But how about your office and safe?"

"There you have me," Hoffenstall admitted, sounding worried.

"Maybe somebody made copies of my keys and sold them to the gang?"

"That's impossible. I'm the only one who has a key to my private office or the safe, and I always carry the keys on my person."

"Always?"

"They never leave my possession. When I take a bath, they hang on a hook behind the bathroom door in my sight. I change them with my clothes and lock them in a deed box, which goes under my bed at night."

"And you take them everywhere you go?" Dusty said. "Hunting, fishing, like that?"

"Of course," agreed Hoffenstall. "As I've said, they never leave my possession no matter where I go."

Which meant, most likely, that he carried them when he went to see the girl at Mama Lola's. If so, and she should be working for the Bad Bunch, at least one person had the opportunity to obtain an impression of the keys, in wax or some other substance, from which duplicates might be accurately copied. Being a keen student of human nature, Dusty decided that he might learn more from Hoffenstall by not mentioning his findings at Mama Lola's place. So he turned the talk to the subject of handling Amesley's business.

"I reckon I'll stay over for a few days and see how things are," Dusty finally said. "It'll give me a chance to see the town."

Hoffenstall did not rise to the hint or offer to show Dusty around. At least not directly.

"If you need accommodation . . ." the banker began.

"Uncle Tim's fixed us up at his place," Dusty replied.

"A group of local business and professional men get together for hunting, fishing, or a game of poker regularly," Hoffenstall said. "I'm one of them and I'd like to invite you along. Tomorrow morning we'll likely be doing some large-mouth-bass fishing, or go out and see if there are any tarpon moving in the river mouth."

"Thanks for the offer. I'll come along. Mind if I bring my *amigos?*"

"Feel free," answered Hoffenstall. "Come around about nine and I'll take you to meet the fellers."

Leaving the banker's home, Dusty returned to Farron's house, where he found the sheriff and his friends waiting. The Kid told Dusty about his visit to the cantina and finished with: "Castro didn't help us any."

"Did you reckon he would?" asked the sheriff.

"I got a mighty winning way with me," drawled the Kid. "Damn it all, though, Tim. If Castro don't know who the Bad Bunch is, I'm certain sure nobody else does."

"Somebody must," Dusty stated. "Even if it's only the members of the gang."

"What're we going to do, Dusty?" asked Mark.

"Stay on here for a spell," Dusty replied. "I want to see what I can learn from Beau's friends."

Although Dusty, Mark, and the Kid spent three more days in Brownsville, they succeeded only in clearing Amesley's friends of being implicated in his death. With the power of Ole Devil's name backing them, most doors around the town opened and the members of the Uptown Fishing, Hunting, and Inside-Straight Club made them welcome. Hard questioning brought about the certainty that Amesley died at a member of the bank-robbing gang's hands, for it eliminated every club member as a suspect. Even Hoffenstall came through clean. While the possibility that he arranged the robbery of his own bank had occurred to Dusty, investigation showed that Hoffenstall lost far more than he could have hoped to gain.

Making a more detailed interrogation of Mama Lola's staff added little to the sum total of knowledge. While her girls described their missing associate, they could add little more information. None had ever seen the girl showing special interest in any one man, other than the banker; nor did she appear to have any friends, male or female, who might be members of, or messengers for, the Bad Bunch.

Satisfied that they could do and learn nothing more in

Brownsville, Dusty gave the order to return to the Rio Hondo. If nothing else, Tim Farron had one thing to be thankful for. Castro's cantina stood empty and deserted, its owner having disappeared without a trace and the clientele scattered until they learned whether he spread around guilty secrets before leaving.

On the evening of their return, the trio followed the usual procedure and gathered in Ole Devil's study to tell the rancher of their activities. Seated around the comfortable, gun-decorated room, each member of the floating outfit went through his findings and gave his conclusions. Betty Hardin and Belle Boyd completed the group and listened with the same intent interest as shown by Ole Devil. At last the rancher nodded grimly.

"You handled things just right," he said.

"And it was the Bad Bunch who killed Beau?" asked Betty.

"Everything points that way," Dusty agreed. "What do you know about them, Belle?"

"Only of their reputation," Belle replied. "So far they haven't committed any crime that puts them under our jurisdiction."

At that time the U.S. Secret Service handled matters affecting the internal security of the nation—spying by foreign powers or treason—and the various aspects of counterfeiting. They did little in the matter of general crime, and many years would pass before the robbery of a bank ranked as a federal crime. However Dusty did not doubt that the girl, or her organization, possessed excellent sources of information. So did the Kid, if it came to a point, and he learned nothing from them.

"Do you think your outfit could learn who the Bad Bunch are?" asked Betty.

"I don't know," admitted Belle. "From what I've heard, there's brains, ability, and organization behind them."

"That's for sure," Dusty said. "The usual run of

owlhoots would've been spending their loot and have given themselves away before now."

"Tell me everything you know about them, Dusty," Belle suggested.

"It's not much at all, Belle," Dusty replied. "Just things lawmen we know write to tell Pappy."

Thinking back on the various reports he had seen concerning the Bad Bunch, Dusty told the girl everything he could remember. During their two assignments, he had formed a good opinion of Belle's abilities and figured that she might be able to make helpful suggestions.

At last Dusty finished and Belle sat silently for a time. Then she nodded.

"There's a pattern in the way they work," she said. "They always hit a bank in a large town. . . ."

"That's where the money'd be," drawled the Kid.

"Did you think that out all by yourself?" Betty scoffed.

"I mean, there's likely more money in a big town's bank," replied the Kid.

"That doesn't follow, Lon," Belle objected. "I bet your bank in town holds as much money as any in a big town."

"Only we'd be more likely to notice strangers in Polveroso than, say in Austin or Houston," Dusty put in.

"There's that," Belle agreed. "They always set fire to some building to draw folks, and more particularly peace officers, from the vicinity of the bank while they raid it, and they always raid at night."

"And on a night when the law's got something extra on hand," Dusty said, driving his left fist into the palm of his right hand. "They hit Austin on the Fourth of July. Took the bank in San Antone on the night of the big prizefight and there were the two Yankee ironclads in Brownsville to keep the law occupied."

"What've we been using for heads, Dusty?" asked Mark with a wry grin.

"Don't blame yourselves," Belle said. "I'm on the outside looking in. You've been too close to the actual problem and too busy to think on it."

"There's one thing you're all forgetting," Ole Devil remarked. "The way the Bad Bunch never leave living witnesses. That could mean only one thing. They're men who'd be recognized; prominent men, maybe."

"It could be," admitted Dusty. "The money never shows after they take it, and if they've some honest business, they'd be able to pass or use it without anybody guessing."

"But who . . ." began Betty.

"You've got us there," Dusty replied. "Unless—"

"Unless it was somebody Beau Amesley knew real well," Ole Devil finished. "Somebody he'd never suspect of being involved in a robbery. A friend."

"One of that sporting club," Mark concluded. "Any one of them could have come up to Beau and used a knife on him before he suspected it."

"Beau'd started to take out his sword, unscrewed the handle, but didn't pull the blade," the Kid said. "Damn it, if I thought—"

"Let's not go off half-cocked," Belle warned. "You're building up a strong case on mighty flimsy evidence. There's nothing to prove any of the club are involved in this business."

"Miss Boyd's right on that, Dustine," Ole Devil stated. "In fact you-all proved pretty well that they couldn't have been."

"So they prepared a mighty strong alibi," Dusty said. "You're right, sir, we've no proof. Unless we find some, that is."

"How?" asked the rancher.

"The easiest way. By catching the Bad Bunch on the job."

"Trust my dear cousin to pick the easiest way," sniffed Betty.

"It's possible," commented Belle. "All we have to do is find a big town that has a celebration or some such event, then go there and keep our eyes open."

"You mean like over to Fort Worth at the end of next month," Dusty remarked. "They're holding the Tarrant County Fair there."

"Which same there'll be folks spilling out at the seams and whooping it up until the dog's shot and the last pup's been hung," Mark went on. "And there'll be money bursting out of the banks for room. Only, will the Bad Bunch have time to set things up by then?"

"They've hit at three-week intervals before now," Belle pointed out. "What do we do, Dusty, inform the local law?"

"Not until we're sure," Dusty answered. "Beau Amesley was a good friend. I'd like to see to his killer myself."

"I'll go along with that," Ole Devil said. "Go up there, Dustine. Take Mark and Lon. Get the Bad Bunch."

"May I come along?" Belle asked. "I may be able to help."

"Why don't you go, too, Betty?" asked Ole Devil. "Then if we should be right about the Uptown Sporting Club, they'll maybe think the floating outfit's only come for the celebrations."

"Only we don't be doing no celebrating happen we've got a bossy she-male trailing along," drawled the Kid.

Coming to her feet, Betty advanced and stood over the Kid. She smiled in her sweetest manner and asked, "Now, who'd you mean by that, Loncey dear?"

"Why, not sweet, lovable, good-natured li'l ole you, for sure," replied the Kid. "And I sure didn't mean a gal who kicks as good as Belle."

"How'd you like that, Belle?" Betty inquired.

"All tricky and treacherous," Belle replied. "He's still a mean border smuggler at heart."

"Which same I never knew he had one," sniffed Betty, and glared at Mark. "And what do we hear from the gentleman from the Big Bend?"

"Don't you go abusing the hired help, gal," warned Mark. "Or I'll write to my congressman."

"Go ahead," dared Betty. "He's my uncle."

"Whyn't you bunch go play mumblety-peg in the stable?" demanded Dusty.

"Watch your mouth, cousin dear," Betty told him. "Tommy taught me a trick that you don't know."

In addition to teaching Dusty the ancient Japanese fighting arts, Tommy Okasi had given Betty a very thorough grounding in jiu-jitsu and karate, at both of which the girl showed considerable proficiency.

Ole Devil brought the meeting to a more serious level. "About Garret, Dustine," he said.

"I'd near on forgotten him," admitted Dusty. "Tommy told me that he's near on ready for getting on his feet again. Did he tell you what brought him here?"

"Like we figured, Jules Murat's forming a Ranger company. He sent Garret here to talk things over with us, see if we'd any suggestions for him."

"And those two fellers we shot?" asked Mark.

"Garret doesn't know," Ole Devil replied. "He figures, and I'm inclined to agree, that they bushwhacked him with robbery in mind."

"There's something else, Dusty," Betty put in. "Danny's going along to join Jules Murat's company."

"What's Pappy say about that?" Dusty said.

"He's leaving it to Danny."

"Danny's a good peace officer, Dusty," Mark commented. "And Jules's going to need all he can get of them."

Already working as their father's deputy, Dusty's younger brother Danny possessed a good knowledge of practical law enforcement. Tough, smart, handy with a gun, Danny ought to be a useful addition to the newly formed Texas Rangers. With work as ranch *segundo* and calls on his services as a member of the floating outfit, Dusty could not join Murat. Probably Danny felt that one of the family ought to be represented in the state's fight to bring back law and order.

"That means Danny'll be going to Fort Worth to join Jules," Dusty remarked.

"He leaves in three days," Ole Devil confirmed.

"Maybe Jules'll let him stay on, then," Dusty went on. "He can keep his eyes and ears open and may learn something."

"We'll put it to them both," Ole Devil replied. "Well, I'm for bed; but you can do what you want."

"Good night, sir," Dusty answered, and looked at the others. "How about you bunch?"

"I'm hungry," Mark stated, eyeing the girls in a suggestive manner.

"And me," the Kid agreed. "Got some thinking to do. Which same I think a heap better full of food."

"Is *think* the word you want?" asked Betty, and kissed her grandfather lightly on the cheek. "Good night, sir."

After the rancher left the room, Betty and Belle fetched milk and biscuits from the kitchen. While eating, the talk went back to the Bad Bunch and its possible connection with the Brownsville Uptown Fishing, Hunting, and Inside-Straight Club. Much as Dusty hated to think that the jovial bunch who shared food, sport, and fun with him might be involved in crime, he admitted the possibility.

"We'll check on them," he said at last. "Trouble being that we can't telegraph Uncle Tim and ask him to help. If word gets back to those fellers, and they *are* the Bad Bunch, we'll scare them right off."

"Then somebody will have to go to Brownsville and ask," Belle remarked.

"And I know who that somebody'll be," groaned the Kid.

"Can you let me have a hand to help dig the truck garden, Cousin Dusty?" Betty inquired.

"Which same I'd dearly love to go to Brownsville, Cap'n Fog, sir," the Kid went on.

"Why don't you and I go with Lon, Betty?" asked Belle. "It will give him an excuse to be back there, and I've a few contacts who might be able to help."

"That's a right smart idea," Dusty said. "See, Lon, women-folks are good for something."

"*I've* never doubted it," commented Mark. "Some of them can think up a right smart idea, too, once in a while."

"You men don't give women credit for half of the things they can do," Belle told him.

Dusty would remember those words in the near future.

10

FAMILIAR FACES IN FORT WORTH

Fort Worth was, as Mark guessed, bursting at its seams with people. They flocked from all over the state and beyond its borders to join in the proposed celebrations. To ensure a large and profitable crowd's attendance, the city fathers and county commissioners spared no expense in gathering attractions. During the week-long festivities there would be dances—varying from hoedowns to real, formal balls—every night, while each day packed in as much variety of entertainment as possible. Being a cattle town, mainly dependent on cowhands for its revenue, the emphasis naturally fell on sports aimed at facets of range work. There would be horse races, bucking broncs to test the mettle of skilled riders, roping, tying, branding matches. Nor would skill of arms be neglected, with revolver- and rifle-shooting competitions. For the ladies, prizes could be won in sewing, cooking, putting up preserves, and other female achievements. All carried healthy cash prizes as an inducement, which the sponsors of the county fair fondly hoped would be paid for—with a fair margin of profit— by the folks who swarmed into town. The culmination of the fair would be on Saturday, with the finals of the major contests during the day and a grand prize giving at a dance that ought to last all night.

Arriving on Monday afternoon of the fair week, Dusty's party found accommodation with some of the small Texan's kinfolk. Leaving the girls to settle in, Dusty, Mark, and the Kid went in search of Danny Fog. Picking up the trail at the hotel room, which served Captain Jules Murat as an unsuspected office, the trio followed it to find Danny among a party of celebrating cowhands and to all appearances one of them.

Danny took after his father, being tall, wide shouldered, blond headed. While good-looking, he was not handsome enough to catch the eye and be noticeable in a crowd, a useful asset for a peace officer. Although now a Texas Ranger, he wore neither uniform nor badge. In fact he looked just like any other cowhand in town for a spree. Around his waist hung a gun belt. The right-side Army Colt pointed its stag-horn butt to the rear, but the one at the left hung handle forward, a method often practiced by men who lacked the ability to shoot well with the left hand yet wanted a second revolver readily available.

"Hey, Brother Dusty!" Danny whooped, and slapped the cowhand at his side on the back. "Will you just look who-all's here, Tracey."

Swinging around, the second cowhand gave a broad, drunken-appearing grin. He, too, wore cowhand clothes and belted a low-hanging Army Colt. Growing a neat moustache had not altered Tracey Prince so much that Dusty failed to recognize him.

"Why, howdy, Cap'n Dusty," he greeted. "You-all just in time for a drink."

"Anytime's a good time for one," Dusty replied. "Let's go get one and a bite to eat."

"Let me get the drinks in, Dusty," Mark offered, and

turned to the waiting bartender. "Set 'em up for the gents here and take something for yourself, friend."

Watched by admiring eyes, for he was very much a hero to the young Texas cowhands, Dusty strolled off with his brother toward a table at the rear of the room. Collecting drinks for the party, the Kid and Prince followed while Mark stayed behind to prevent other members of Danny's group following.

"I see you joined the Rangers, Tracey," Dusty remarked as they sat down.

"Sure, Cap'n. I was holding down a deputy town marshal's star and Cap'n Murat made me the offer. Pay's better and the work's likely to be better, too."

After recovering from his wound, Tracey Prince drifted away from the Rio Hondo. At first his search for the abducted girl threatened to send him down the same trail as Wes Hardin, Bill Longley, and other fast-handed Texans forced into one killing too many. Good with a gun, Prince prowled the Texas ranges for two years and then finally settled down as a peace officer. Dusty heard of him over the years but their paths never crossed. One thing the small Texan learned was that Prince tended to rely too much on his gun when making an arrest. While Dusty believed in taking no chances, he admitted that on occasion, if rumor be true, Prince drew and shot for mighty flimsy reasons.

Dusty mentioned none of his thoughts, figuring it to be none of his business. Certainly Jules Murat must have faith in Prince, or he would not have taken the young man into his company.

On sitting at the table, Danny and Prince lost their pose of cheery near-drunkenness. Danny grinned amiably at his brother.

"You sure handed me a dilly," he said.

"How come?" Dusty asked.

" 'Keep your eyes peeled,' you said. 'Watch out for

anybody who looks suspicious and check on any of that Brownsville bunch who might come in!' "

"So?"

"So look at all the folks. They're swarming in from all sides and down off the high country."

"I told you not to be a tin star," scoffed the Kid.

"Only took it hoping I get 'round to jailing you," Danny told him. "Well, I prowled and I've watched. I've kept both eyes open awake and asleep. I've watched standing, sitting, lying—"

"If you'd got eyes in your butt end, you could've watched folks behind you, too," the Kid pointed out. "We've all had our hardships. Take me—"

"Not with both arms loaded down with gold," scoffed Danny. "Anyways, what hardships have you ever had?"

"Well, I done took Betty and Belle down to Brownsville for a visit."

"That's hardship?" asked Prince.

"Damned if they didn't make me get all fancied up, string tie and all, two separate nights," stated the aggrieved Kid.

"That's hardship," conceded Prince.

"Did you see anything by all that watching, Brother Danny?" Dusty put in.

"McKie, Colonel Mayne, Jeffers, the gunsmith and Judge Noire arrived last night and put up at the Cattlemen's Hotel."

"Know anything about them, Cap'n?" Prince asked.

"Lon learned some. McKie made his money running slaves before the war and breaking the Yankee blockade in it. He's thought to have banked his money in Nassau or Bermuda and didn't lose it when the war ended."

"There weren't many saints slave-running or on blockade breakers," Danny commented.

"McKie was tough, all right," the Kid answered. "They used to call him 'Bowie' McKie on account of him being so good with one."

"Then—" Danny began.

"We thought of *that* already," Dusty drawled. "Colonel Mayne was in the Quartermaster Corps, him and Judge Noire used to travel around Texas on purchasing commissions for the army. Which means that they'll have contacts in damned near every big town."

"How about Jeffers?" asked Danny.

"He's a decent gunsmith, but a better locksmith according to what I learned," answered the Kid. "They do say he can open any lock ever made."

"Then—" Danny commenced.

"And we've thought of that, too," interrupted Dusty. "They all do a fair bit of traveling, so do most of that bunch. Some of the trips tie in with the dates of Bad Bunch jobs."

"So what do we do?" demanded Prince.

"Nothing," Dusty replied.

"Nothing?" yelped two voices.

"I sure admire fellers with poker faces," drawled the Kid, eyeing Danny and Prince sardonically. "Whyn't you pair get up and do a hoedown 'round the table?"

"Danged Injun," sniffed Danny.

"We wasn't figuring on you wanting to sit back and let 'em do their robbery, Cap'n Dusty," Prince went on.

"Now listen to me," Dusty growled. "Jules Murat told me to put you pair onto this Bad Bunch chore and work with you. So we'll play it my way."

"It's your game, Dusty," Danny answered, and Prince grunted confirmation.

"Then this's how we play it. First thing, there's no proof that those fellers are the Bad Bunch. . . ."

"You just told us—" Prince began.

"All we have against them is circumstances," Dusty pointed out. "They've all had real good reasons for being away from Brownsville on business or for sport every time they went. Every one of them has a profitable business to account for where he gets his money. So we can't handle them like they're a bunch of owlhoots with pictures on every post office wall in Texas."

"What do we do, Dusty?" asked Danny.

"We watch them. See who they meet, if they show interest in any particular bank or other place that holds a lot of money. Until we know something, that's all we do."

"It'll be slow work," Prince remarked.

"Slow, boring, and maybe for no reason," admitted Dusty. "Handled any other way, it'd blow back in our faces. If they are the Bad Bunch, we'll scare them off. If not, the Rangers'll have some mighty influential folks riled at them."

"That shouldn't worry us," sniffed Prince.

"It damned well *should!*" barked Dusty. "You Rangers are taking on a tough, mean, and dirty job. You'll have enough enemies among the outlaw element without turning folks who might help you against you. Look, Tracey, if you'd like me to ask Jules Murat to take you off—"

"You never steered me wrong in the war, Cap'n," Prince cut in. "And I reckon you're right now. How do we play things?"

"We'll say that they are the Bad Bunch and work that way, as long as we work easy," Dusty drawled. "Mayne and Noire are the best bets for gathering information about where to hit. Jeffers will handle the locks and safe and McKie stand lookout. So right now we concentrate on the first two. Between us, we'll watch them every waking and sleeping hour of the day. If they are going to make a move, we must learn where and work out when."

The surveillance proved far easier than Dusty imagined. That evening he met the four men at a party. They greeted him warmly and insisted that he join them at the theater and arranged to meet up with him in the morning so as to make use of his cowhand knowledge while making bets on the steer roping. If the men planned to commit robbery, they gave no sign of it and made no attempt to cultivate anybody who might supply information.

Of the four, McKie tended to go his own way most. A man self-made in a hard and rough school, he often drifted into a different circle than his friends. So much so that Dusty told Danny and Prince to watch the man, leaving the floating outfit to cover the others.

For three days the watching went on, with Dusty growing more sure that they wasted their time. Belle Boyd saw contacts, coming up with minor information, which she passed on to the Rangers, but learned nothing of the Bad Bunch.

Three days of comparative inactivity made Prince chafe at the bit; especially as, due to Belle's information, other members of the company made two spectacular arrests of known outlaws attracted by the chance of easy money at the fair.

"Damn it all, Danny," he complained as they stood at the bar of a saloon on the third night. "This here's a no-good chore."

"Likely," replied Danny tolerantly. "At least we've seen some of the sights around town."

"Sights!" snorted Prince. "Buck Lemming and Sandy Gartrees pulled in the Pitt brothers and nailed Dude Rankin's hide to the wall. All we've done is stand around and look."

"We get paid for it," Danny said, and looked up at the balcony.

They had followed McKie to the saloon and watched him go upstairs to one of the rooms lining the balcony, where a large-stake poker game was in progress. Due to the high stakes involved, neither Ranger could follow McKie and join the game without arousing his suspicions. So they stayed in the bar, stretching out their drinks and waiting to see what developed. It seemed that the game would last for some time as a waiter took in a tray with a load of sandwiches on it.

While speaking, Danny saw the door open and the waiter backed out. A napkin hung over his right hand, covering it completely and he drew the door closed with his left. Danny felt struck by the caution with which the man left the room, and his suspicions increased as the other turned a key in the door's lock.

"That waiter's acting mighty strange!" Danny told Prince. "Let's go over and have a talk to him."

"It'll beat standing here," Prince grunted. "We can't even get drunk."

Turning casually, the two men walked toward the bottom of the stairs. Danny watched the waiter coming down, his hand still hidden under the napkin draped over his forearm. To all appearances everything was normal enough. If anything should be wrong, they ought to be able to take the man with no trouble.

"Watch him, Danny!" Prince yelled, shooting out his left hand to shove his companion to one side.

At the same moment Prince's right hand dropped and scooped the Army Colt from his holster. Even as he staggered, Danny saw a mixture of shock and anger cross the waiter's face and he started to raise the napkin-covered hand. Flame ripped from the barrel of Prince's Colt and a .44 bullet drove into the waiter's chest. He rocked back under the impact, ankles striking the step behind him and causing him to lose his balance. Sliding away, the napkin exposed a short-barreled Webley Bulldog revolver. Again Prince fired, acting correctly under the circumstances, and the second bullet caused the man to release his weapon; then he slid slowly down the stairs.

"Saw the gun just in time," Prince commented.

While Danny had hoped to take the man alive, he could hardly blame Prince for acting in such a manner. There was no time to waste in discussing it, however.

Going upstairs fast, Danny saw the room's door burst open and a man emerged cautiously. After glancing in each direction along the balcony, the man spoke over his shoulder and came out. McKie and several other players followed.

"See you got the bastard, young feller," McKie said, looking down to where a small crowd gathered around the body of the waiter.

"What'd he done?" asked Danny, although willing to guess.

"Held up our game," McKie replied. "Come in with a tray of sandwiches and next thing we knew he'd got a gun on us. Made us all lie down on the floor, allowed there was a feller across the street with a rifle lined on us and two more on the balcony here."

"There weren't any out here," Danny assured him, and stepped cautiously into the room. Ignoring the signs of the game, he went to the window and looked out. The saloon faced one of Fort Worth's better hotels, but he saw no sign of a rifle or man in the room opposite.

"Say, you're Dusty Fog's brother, aren't you?" McKie asked as Danny emerged.

"That's me," Danny agreed. "I'd best go across the street and make sure that feller's not up there."

Joining Prince at the foot of the stairs, Danny told the other his intention. On their way to the door, they met a deputy town marshal. Fortunately he knew them to be Rangers and wasted no time in asking questions. Leaving the deputy to handle things in the saloon, Danny and Prince crossed the street and entered the hotel. Clearly the desk clerk did not regard them as possible roomers, the place being of temperance persuasion and not the kind frequented by cowhands. However he knew a Ranger's star-in-the-circle badge when he saw one and answered Danny's request for information promptly.

"Third room from the left at the front?" he said.

"That's a Miss Cosethorpe and her secretary. She's a writer from back East."

"Are they up in the room now?" Danny asked.

"I-I think so."

"We'd best go and see," stated Prince, and continued, as they went upstairs, "How do we play it, Danny?"

"Knock on the door and wait for it to open. If there was a feller inside covering the game, he'll likely be gone by now."

"If he's not . . ."

"We're in trouble. He'll have the women in there with him."

On reaching the door they required, Danny and Prince exchanged glances. Neither of them underestimated the danger and they took precautions. Instead of standing in front of the door, they stood against the wall on either side of it. Then Danny reached around and knocked. If a bullet came through the door, aimed at where the knocker might be expected to stand, it would miss them.

No bullet came. Instead, after a brief wait, the door opened. Just about the most homely girl Danny had ever seen peered out through steel-rimmed glasses. Dull, lifeless-looking mousy brown hair, taken back in a severe style, framed a pale face with puffy cheeks. A plain black traveling dress effectively prevented any hint of her figure showing, which might be just as well, Danny concluded, if it matched her face.

Although the girl opened the door calmly enough, it seemed that an expression of surprise—if nothing worse —flickered over her face as she looked at Prince. Then she turned her eyes to the badge Danny held before her.

"We're Texas Rangers, ma'am," Danny told her. "Is everything all right in your room?"

"Why shouldn't it be?" she asked. She had a pleasant

voice, but its effect was spoiled by the revelation of two black gaps among her teeth.

At Danny's side, Prince stiffened slightly and stared hard at the girl. He opened his mouth as if to say something, then closed it again and allowed Danny to do the talking.

"Can we come in, ma'am?"

"What is it, Clarise?" called a deep, feminine voice from inside the room.

"There're two Texas Rangers outside, Miss Cosethorpe. They want to come in."

"Do they?" growled the voice.

A shape behind the girl; big, menacing, but undoubtedly female. Not that the second occupant of the room proved to be any oil painting as far as looks were concerned. Dressed in a severe style, the woman glared at the Rangers in a manner that drove a chill through them both. However, Danny recovered fast and, once more showing his badge, told her of the holdup and story about the man with a rifle being in her room.

"There is no man in here," boomed Miss Cosethorpe. "Come in and look for yourselves if you wish."

Entering the room, Danny looked around him. Not that he expected the man to be present. In fact Danny would have been willing to bet that any man who tried to force an entry to *that* room very rapidly came around to regretting his action. After a quick look around, he thanked the woman for her cooperation and nudged Prince, who stood staring at the girl. Prince's attitude surprised Danny. While the other still retained his girl-chasing ways, it hardly seemed likely that one so homely would attract him.

"Reckon we ought to try the other rooms?" Danny asked as they returned to the passage.

"Huh?" grunted Prince, directing another stare at the door as it closed.

"The other rooms, those on either side of this one,"

explained Danny. "Not that I reckon there's anybody we want in them. That was the only room with a view into the saloon."

"You're likely right," Prince answered distantly.

"Come on, Tracey," Danny said with a grin. "You sure as hell couldn't be struck on *that* gal."

"It couldn't be," Prince answered, and shook his head. "Maybe we'd best go look in the rooms on each side, Danny."

"You could be right at that," Danny replied.

A check on the neighboring rooms failed to produce the rifleman, and by the time the Rangers reached the street, Prince acted as he normally did. On their return to the saloon, Danny questioned the players in the game. Due to his questioning and a smart piece of deductive work, Danny proved one of the men in the game worked with the robber. By the time the affair reached its logical conclusion, Prince's unusual behavior had passed from Danny's mind.

11

A FRESH SUSPECT

While Danny Fog and Prince handled their first assignment as Rangers, Dusty's party also worked on the search for the Bad Bunch. At the time his brother arrested the second member of the holdup team, Dusty stood talking with a couple of ranchers at the bar of the newly formed Cattlemen's Association ball. While Mark, the Kid, Betty, and Belle, the latter wearing a natural-looking blond wig over her short dark hair, danced, Dusty preferred to remain on the sidelines and discuss the cattle business with other interested parties. Belle attracted Dusty's attention and gave a signal that caused him to excuse himself and walk over to join her.

"What do you think about Mayne's party, Dusty?" she asked as he collected a glass of punch for her.

"I think we're wasting our time," Dusty answered frankly.

"It's possible," Belle admitted. "By the way, Pierre du Pont's in town."

"And who's he?"

"A pretty smart eastern criminal. A master hand with locks and safes."

"We'd best tell Jules—" Dusty began.

"Or watch him ourselves," Belle interrupted. "Jules Murat has enough on his hands right now without that. And anyway, du Pont dabbles in counterfeiting often enough for my organization to want to nail his hide to the wall."

"I want the Bad Bunch," Dusty pointed out.

"There's nothing to stop du Pont being part of it. He's smart enough to fix the jobs, and he's been working Texas for some time."

"I'd sooner have him as boss of the Bad Bunch than one of the Brownsville crowd," Dusty remarked. "All right, we'll watch him, if you point him out."

"That's easy enough," smiled Belle and nodded across the room. "He's here."

Following the direction of the girl's gaze, Dusty saw a medium-sized, handsome man dressed in faultless good taste. Clearly fully at home in good society, the man approached the hostess of the ball, bowed, and introduced himself.

"Does he know you?" Dusty asked.

"I doubt it," Belle replied. "I never worked in his neighborhood. Heard of him from one of our people who picked up the tip from an informer."

"If he's that well known, somebody ought to have placed him as one of the Bad Bunch," Dusty said.

"Unless he's playing real tricky," the girl answered. "Doing just enough of his usual work so that nobody does connect him. He works with two regular partners; one of them is said to be good with a knife."

"Let's go get to know him," drawled Dusty, and took the girl's arm. Acting as if merely crossing the dance floor, they approached du Pont and their hostess.

As Dusty expected to happen, the woman stopped him. "Ah, Count," she said. "You must meet Captain Fog. Dusty, this is Count Alexi of Bordeaux."

"My pleasure, sir," Dusty answered.

"The count plans to enter the cattle business, Dusty," the hostess went on. "Perhaps you could give him a few helpful hints?"

"I'll surely try," promised Dusty, and the woman drifted away.

During the remainder of the evening, Dusty talked with du Pont and introduced him to a number of people. Although not giving any sign of noticing, Dusty saw that du Pont showed greatest interest when meeting one of the town's bankers. Before the evening ended, the handsome Creole had invitations to visit from the presidents of the town's three banks.

"Who was the dude?" Mark asked as he, the Kid, and Dusty escorted the two girls home that night.

"A French Creole owlhoot, according to Belle," Dusty replied.

"And a real smart one," the girl went on. "I'd say he was more likely to be one of the Bad Bunch than the men from Brownsville."

"Only him being smart doesn't explain how he, or one of his bunch, could walk up and knife Beau Amesley," Dusty pointed out.

"It doesn't," Belle agreed. "What do we do, Dusty?"

"Watch him and his bunch," the small Texan replied.

"Not more of that," groaned Mark.

Watching du Pont proved far easier than expected. Next morning the man came around and offered to escort the two girls to the horse races. Seeing him in the company of Betty Hardin and her "cousin," after having been introduced to him by Captain Dusty Fog, the three bankers tossed aside any doubts they might have harbored about du Pont. At no time did he offer to contact his two partners, but spent all the morning and afternoon with Dusty's party.

During the early afternoon a snag arose to Dusty's plans. Over at Dallas the marshal arrested a man he suspected of being Hamilton White, wanted for robbing stagecoaches. As the man insisted that he was not White and worked for the OD Connected, the marshal telegraphed Murat to request assistance in making the identification. As Danny knew all the OD Connected crew, Murat told him to ride over to Dallas. The chore did not call for two men, which left Prince to carry on watching McKie's movements.

Later that evening Dusty's party went to the theater accompanied by du Pont, Mayne, Noire, and Jeffers. McKie had roamed off once more, with Prince following him. As far as Dusty knew, du Pont still had not contacted his men.

While laughing at the antics of a comedian, Dusty felt a hand touch his arm. Turning, he found Jules Murat standing behind him. The Ranger captain dressed fashionably and looked part of the company in that section of the theater, but the expression on his dark, handsome face warned Dusty that all was far from well. Rising, Dusty excused himself to the others. He saw a flicker of some emotion cross du Pont's face on seeing Murat and then withdrew with the other.

"What's up, Jules?" Dusty asked when beyond du Pont's hearing.

"Tracey Prince's been killed."

"How?"

"With a knife. Slit open like a gutted deer."

"We'll come with you," Dusty decided.

"Trouble, Dusty?" asked du Pont as the small Texan returned to the party.

"A mite. Will you see the girls home, Alexi?"

"Of course. Unless I can help . . . ?"

"It's not much. Mark, Lon, and I can handle it."

"Then we'll attend to the ladies," promised du Pont, and the other three nodded in agreement.

Dusty, Mark, and the Kid walked with Murat through the streets and around to the rear of a livery barn. By the corral lay Prince's body; a small group of peace officers—Rangers and members of the marshal's office —stood to one side. Going forward, the newcomers looked down at the body and the Kid bent to make a closer examination in the light of a lantern.

"Whoever did it knew how to handle a knife real well," he concluded.

"But how did he get close enough to do it?" Murat said. "Tracey was a good peace officer, but just a shade too quick to get his gun out. I can't see him letting anybody come up with a knife in hand."

"Who found the body?" asked Dusty, thinking back to how Amesley died.

"The barn's swamper. Tracey was just alive when the feller found him."

"Did he see anybody?"

"Nope. Tracey must have been lying there and bleeding for some time."

"I don't suppose Tracey said anything?" Mark said.

"Nothing to help us. Like I said, he must have been near on gone and rambling in his mind. He said something about an angel."

"An angel?" repeated Dusty, wondering why the words should mean something to him and failing to connect them to anything he could remember.

"Like I said," Murat replied. "Tracey must have been rambling. He was one of my men, Dusty. I want the bastard who killed him."

"We'll do what we can to help you," Dusty promised. "A good place to start would be by finding McKie."

"Let's go find him, then," Murat growled.

Being the only men present who knew McKie, Dusty, Mark, and the Kid split up to go in search of the man. Murat watched them go and then turned back to the business of trying to find a witness to Prince's murder. Using their knowledge of McKie's tastes in entertainment, the three Texans had a start in their search. As Dusty walked toward the saloon where McKie had played poker the previous night and where the high-stake game continued, he saw a man and woman approaching whom he knew.

"Howdy, Cap'n Fog," the man greeted. "If you're looking for Miss Blaze, we just saw her going down toward the Bayswater livery barn."

"Thanks," Dusty replied, wondering what caused Belle Boyd to leave the theater. "She's likely gone to see if there's a buggy to hire for a moonlight picnic."

"With the count?" smiled the woman. "He went down there just before your cousin."

"I'm just going to chaperon them," Dusty said, wanting to stop any gossip. "If you see any of the floating outfit, could you tell them that we're trying the Bayswater barn?"

"Sure, Cap'n," grinned the man. "The count'll make a right smart catch."

"You could be right at that," Dusty drawled, and walked away, leaving the couple believing that no more than an advantageous courtship lay behind the girl's following du Pont to the barn.

While Dusty wore a town shirt, tie, and trousers, he retained his gun belt. Far too many people had reason to want to meet him unarmed for risks to be taken. He did not trouble to draw his guns while approaching the barn, as that would be a clear warning to du Pont that he expected trouble.

Dusty saw nothing of either Belle or du Pont as he approached the barn. Like most such places, it was illuminated by lanterns so that customers might leave or collect their horses without disturbing the owner. Advancing cautiously toward the front doors, he heard voices from inside.

"Why, I just naturally followed you for a chance to be alone with you," Belle was saying.

"And for no other reason?" asked du Pont.

"Well, I did think that you liked me—"

"Stand still, feller!" rasped a voice from Dusty's left.

Turning his head slightly, Dusty saw a blocky shape move out of the shadows and approach him. A dull metallic glint hinted at a revolver in the man's hand and as he drew closer Dusty saw it to be a Deane and Adams Navy model with its barrel cut short for easy concealment. Not much taller than Dusty, the man wore a cheap town suit, derby hat, and would weigh a fair bit heavier than the small Texan.

Even as Dusty prepared to make a move, he realized that a shot would warn du Pont and endanger Belle. While the girl wore one of her special skirts, she might not be in a position to slip free of it. Nor did the approaching man offer any chance of reversing their positions, for he came to a halt well clear of Dusty.

"Unbuckle the gun belt," ordered the man.

Like all good military leaders, Dusty knew when to surrender and obey. He sensed that the man could handle a gun well enough to make disobedience dangerous and, having Belle to consider, unbuckled the belt, then allowed it to drop to the ground at his feet.

"What is it, Raoul?" called du Pont.

"Caught a feller snooping around," replied the man.

"Bring him in."

Entering the barn, Dusty saw du Pont standing facing Belle. Behind the girl, holding her by the arms, was a tall, lean, city-dressed tough with a knife-scarred face that looked as mean as sin. Moving closer, Raoul did not touch Dusty with his revolver and had not troubled to bring in the small Texan's gun belt.

"Ah, Dusty," greeted du Pont. "As they say in the stupid melodramas we see, the plot thickens."

"I can't say that I like this, Count," Dusty replied. "Finding Cousin Sarah here with you and you having one of your hired help mauling her."

"Please," du Pont smiled. "The young lady may be

your cousin, but I doubt if either of you regard me
merely as a possible husband for her."

"Why, Cousin Dusty!" Belle gasped, looking as innocent as a newborn baby. "I surely don't know what the
count's talking about."

"Come now, Miss Blaze," du Pont replied. "This na-
ive little country girl sits badly on you. It might have
worked, but I saw the Kid watching my room at the
hotel late this afternoon."

"You want for me to cut her up, maybe, boss?" asked
the man behind Belle.

"Not yet, Henri," du Pont answered. "I'm curious to
know where I went wrong, for they know I am not the
count of Bordeaux. It can't be because of wanted post-
ers. I'm not known in Texas."

"Somebody knew you," Dusty pointed out.

"And I want to know who it was," du Pont told him.

"You heard the boss, runt," growled Raoul, stepping
closer and lifting his revolver's barrel toward the back
of Dusty's head. "If you or the gal don't talk, you're
dead."

Which proved a mighty foolish thing to do. Lulled
into a sense of false security by Dusty's small size and
insignificant appearance, Raoul gave the Texan the
awaited chance. Even the weapon held by the man,
ideal though it might be for carrying concealed on the
person, helped Dusty make his move.

Knowing something of Dusty's ways, Belle guessed
that the moment for action had arrived. When making
his suggestion about cutting the girl, Henri took his
right hand from her arm. Like his companion, he failed
to realize the danger. Already Belle's hand rested on
her waistband, ready to free it. A slight nod from Dusty
as the revolver lifted toward his head gave her the tip to
move.

Down slid the skirt, and as it landed Belle raised her
right foot clear of it. She drove back the foot, spiking the

high heel of her boot into Henri's shin bone with sickening force. A howl broke from the man and he released Belle's other arm. Like a flash she pivoted into a *chassé croisé* kick, which stabbed into Henri's ribs and sent him staggering aside.

The moment Belle released her skirt, Dusty made his opening move. Given the momentary distraction caused by the girl's disrobing, Dusty took his chance. He knew the Deane and Adams revolver to be double action, with no spur on the hammer so that trigger pressure along could fire it, and figured that gave him just a split second longer in which to act.

Ducking down and twisting his torso around, Dusty threw up his right arm to strike Raoul's wrist and deflect the gun. Continuing to turn, Dusty caught the man's wrist with his right hand. Before Raoul realized fully what had happened, his revolver no longer lined on Dusty and strong fingers prevented him from turning it back. Whipping his left hand up and across toward his right shoulder, Dusty lashed it around. He used the *urekan*, back fist, of karate and drove the projecting knuckle of the second finger into the philtrum, the collection of nerves in the center of the upper lip and just under the nose.

Although unable to deliver a blow hard enough to incapacitate Raoul, Dusty sent enough pain through him to make him relax his hold on the revolver. Sliding his right hand down from Raoul's wrist, Dusty gripped the Deane and Adams by the chamber and started to twist it free.

Once Henri had released her, Belle sprang forward and aimed a kick at du Pont's belly. Although as surprised as his men at the girl's action, du Pont recovered fast. He also showed a rapid grasp of the situation and knowledge of savate. Drawing back a pace to avoid the girl's kick, he hooked his right foot under her leg from its outer side and heaved. Thrown off balance, Belle

staggered away and du Pont whirled toward Dusty.
Leaping forward, du Pont brought up a kick, which
collided with the revolver and tore it from Dusty's
grasp.

Releasing Raoul, Dusty lunged at du Pont. For once
the small Texan underestimated an enemy. Grabbing
Dusty's shirt front, du Pont fell backward and rammed
a foot into the small Texan's stomach. Hauled off balance, Dusty felt his feet leave the ground and the sensation of flying through the air, which always came when
caught by such a throw. As he sailed over, propelled by
du Pont's thrusting leg, Dusty prepared to land as softly
as possible. Years of horse riding helped his jiu jitsu
training in the matter of breaking a fall. Allowing his
body to relax, he let his hands and feet take the impact
and cushion his landing.

Wild with rage and pain, Raoul plunged by his boss to
land kneeling at Dusty's side. Thick-fingered hands
lunged at the small Texan's throat and Dusty curled up
his lower body. Out lashed Dusty's left leg, its boot
colliding solidly with Raoul's face. Raoul reared back,
lifted almost to his feet by the boot's impact. Blood
spurted from his nose and he crashed over onto his
rump.

While Dusty met the combined attack, Belle managed to gain control of her staggering body. She saw the
danger that now threatened her as Henri rushed in her
direction. Whipping under his jacket, the man's hand
emerged holding a razor-sharp, spear-pointed push
dagger. While possessing only a four-inch blade, such a
knife in skilled hands worked almost as effectively as a
bowie. From all appearances, Henri had the skill to
make his weapon a deadly threat to Belle's life.

Giving the appearance of fear, Belle twisted away
from the man. Then she flopped forward so that her
hands hit the floor and legs bent under her. The move
came only just in time. Out licked the push dagger, to

pass through where Belle's ribs had been an instant before. Carried forward by the impetus of his slash, Henri could not halt himself. Which proved unfortunate. Balancing on her hands, Belle thrust her legs upward and back. Her feet rammed with considerable force into Henri's advancing body. Breath burst from his lungs, he jackknifed over and shot backward faster than he could handle in his present state. Even as Henri collapsed in a double-over heap, Belle landed back on her feet and stood erect. Before doing anything further, she kicked the knife into the straw of a nearby stall. Then she turned to see how Dusty fared.

Starting to rise, Dusty saw du Pont already up and coming at him. Out lashed the Creole's foot, aimed at Dusty's ribs. Only this time Dusty was ready. Stabbing forward his hands, Dusty intercepted the oncoming leg. His right hand caught the boot, while his left closed on the ankle. As he rose, Dusty gave the trapped leg a twisting heave, which threw du Pont staggering across the barn.

Du Pont caught his balance much sooner than Dusty expected and shot out a fist as the Texan followed him. Going under the blow, Dusty ripped a punch into du Pont's body and clipped his other hand into the man's face. Before he could do more, Dusty felt two hands close on his neck from behind. Shaking his head, du Pont hit Dusty in the face, closing in to take advantage of Raoul's intervention. Bringing up his right foot, Dusty placed it against du Pont's body and thrust the man away. Doing so allowed Dusty to move back against Raoul's grip and caused the man to relax his pressure slightly. Whipping up his hands, Dusty caught Raoul's wrists. Swiftly Dusty pivoted his body to the left and heaved the hands away from his neck. He jerked Raoul's left arm under the man's right and gave a surging heave, which forced the right arm downward. Coming so fast, and with Dusty's considerable strength behind it, the twisting of the arms catapulted Raoul over so that the man crashed down hard on his back.

Already du Pont came back to the attack. Before he could reach Dusty, Belle arrived. Bounding into the air while still some six feet away from du Pont, the girl drew both legs up under her and then shot them out in a thrusting kick. So intent had du Pont been on handling Dusty that he saw the danger too late. Belle's left foot struck his shoulder, but the right collided with the side of his head. The force of the leaping-high kick flung du Pont sideways, and he went down barely conscious. Even as she landed, the girl saw a fresh danger.

"Dusty!" she screamed.

Holding his belly, Henri lurched across to catch up a pitchfork from its place by one of the stalls. With the sharp-pointed weapon in his hands, he swung to charge. Dusty saw the Deane and Adams lying close by and dived forward. Catching up the revolver as he landed, he fired while still on his back. Lead tore into Henri's chest, spun him around, and tumbled him to the ground.

"Hold it!" Dusty barked as Raoul sat up.

Although dazed, Raoul could still think well enough to know the danger. Crossing a man who could handle a strange gun that well was a sure way of getting killed. So the blocky man stayed on the ground and looked to his boss for guidance. Sitting up and shaking his head to clear it, du Pont looked around. He took in the gun Dusty held, Belle's graceful position of savate readiness, and then turned his eyes to where Henri sprawled bleeding.

"All right, Dusty," du Pont said. "We're licked."

"I figured you might be," Dusty replied. "Go get my gun belt from outside, Belle."

Without a thought for her appearance, Belle obeyed. She found the gun belt and collected it, but saw no sign of anybody coming to investigate the shot. On her return, she hung the belt on a stall, handed Dusty the right-hand Colt, and took the Deane from him.

"May I ask what crime I'm supposed to have committed?" du Pont said, kneeling at Henri's side.

"How about having a Ranger killed?" asked Dusty.

"A Rang . . . You're joking, no?"

"That's one thing I'd never joke about."

"I know the Rangers are being organized, but they know nothing of me. Why would I kill one?"

"Not you," corrected Dusty. "That knife artist there."

"Henri? That's impossible. I told him to stay in his room and he always obeys my orders. Can we get a doctor to attend to him? He's not much to look at, but he's loyal. By the by, Raoul was with Henri all evening."

"As soon as I've had some answers," Dusty promised. "Can they prove they've never left the room?"

"Can you, Raoul?" asked du Pont.

"Only way out's by the desk clerk or down a rope from the window, and that'd be facing the Ranchers' Bank," Raoul growled.

"So that's where you aimed to hit," Belle said.

"It was," sighed du Pont. "But as I say, I have committed no crime here."

"How about in Brownsville on the twenty-seventh of last month?" asked Dusty.

"I would have had to be there to do so," du Pont replied.

"And you weren't?"

"No."

"Where were you?" asked Dusty.

"That is my business."

"Go outside and start screaming, Belle," ordered Dusty.

"What's this?" demanded du Pont.

"When the folks come to see why, I'll be hidden in a stall," Dusty said. "I don't reckon you being a 'count' will make any difference to how they treat you when they find you've been mishandling a girl."

A point that du Pont readily understood. He knew enough of western towns to realize that being a distinguished visitor would not save him from the citizens' wrath on finding him in such a position.

"Why Brownsv . . ." he began. "Ah yes. The robbery. I assure you, Dusty, that on the twenty-seventh I was in Austin. And I can prove it. There was a large-stake poker game—in fact some of the players are in town at the moment. Henri was with me. In fact he and Raoul wound up in jail the same night after a saloon fight."

"I think he's telling the truth, Dusty," Belle stated, donning her skirt and starting to tidy up her appearance.

So it proved. Not only did the players in the game confirm du Pont's story, but they cleared McKie, who had never left the game after joining it at six o'clock. Whatever other crimes he might have committed, du Pont was not one of the Bad Bunch.

12

THE BAD BUNCH MAKES A RAID

"Well, we're no nearer to knowing who the Bad Bunch are," the Ysabel Kid remarked as he sat at breakfast with his friends on Saturday morning. "It wasn't McKie or that Creole who knifed young Prince. McKie couldn't have, and that push dagger wouldn't leave a gash like I saw in Prince."

"What's happening about du Pont's bunch?" asked Betty.

"The marshal's holding them in jail and seeing them on Monday's stage," Dusty told her. "There's not a hint of anybody else who might be the Bad Bunch."

"Maybe they aren't here at all," Betty suggested.

"I've a feeling they are," Belle answered. "This kind of setup is just made for them."

"I go along with Belle," Mark drawled. "Don't ask me why. . . ."

"The way Prince was killed tells us they're likely here," Dusty pointed out. "Now all we have to do is figure out where they'll hit."

"There're three banks and the Wells Fargo office to choose from," Betty said.

"Don't forget the county offices," Belle reminded. "In addition to tax money and their general funds, they're holding over nine thousand dollars in prize money for various events."

"Only that'll be gone by evening," Dusty replied. "The Bad Bunch have always hit after dark before this."

"They could change their ways," Belle warned. "Of the four, the county offices would be easiest to take. Its safe is in a ground-floor room at the back—"

"With two men on watch over it twenty-four hours a day until the prize money's gone," Mark pointed out. "Jules fixed that up from the start."

"If they aim to hit that safe, it'll have to be this afternoon," Dusty insisted. "Otherwise there won't be enough money in it to be worthwhile."

"Like you said, the Bad Bunch only hit in the dark," Mark put in.

"Only around the middle of the afternoon near on everybody'll be out watching the finals of the different events," Dusty answered. "I bet there's not a handful of folks in town until evening."

"What do we do then, Dusty?" asked the Kid.

"Take no chances," was the reply. "We'll watch—"

"Where?" prompted Belle, seeing the difficulties as Dusty had.

"Every time so far they've set fire to some place to draw folks away from where they hit," Dusty said. "All four places are pretty close together, down to the south end of town. I'd say they'd pick on the Bayswater livery barn. It's the best place for them and it'd burn real good."

"So?" asked Betty.

"So when they send their man, I want one of us waiting for him."

"At the barn?" Mark inquired.

"Sure. We don't know which place they aim to hit, but

we can near enough bet the Bayswater's where they touch off their fire."

"And if they don't pick that barn?" Belle wanted to know. "Why not ask either Jules or the marshal for men?"

"Because they're both using every man they can spare to cover the banks and watch the crowds out at the events," Dusty replied. "We can't ask them to spare a man for something that may never happen."

"Looks like we'll have to handle it ourselves, then," the Kid commented.

"I'll tell you what, Dusty," Mark drawled. "I'll watch the barn this afternoon while you and Lon take the girls to the races. If nothing happens, we'll all take a place and watch it tonight."

Which only went to prove, Mark told himself for the twentieth time as he sat in a stall at the livery barn, that he talked too much. While the rest of the town enjoyed the finals of various events, he waited for something that might not happen. Fort Worth's streets had the aspect of a ghost town, every business being closed. Even the saloons shut their doors, although the more enterprising carried supplies of liquid refreshments out to the various events in wagons and did a lively trade.

A shadow fell across the open door of the barn and Mark's right hand went automatically toward the butt of the off-side Colt. Then he relaxed as a beautiful blond girl entered. She wore a neat black traveling suit, white blouse, and dainty hat. While fashionable, the clothes gave the impression of a slender, shapely figure without being blatant or making her look the less demure and charming. Despite the warmth of the day, she pandered to fashion by carrying a muff dangling from her left hand. Her eyes went to Mark and surprise flickered across her face; then she smiled and approached him.

"Good afternoon," she said, her voice pleasant and hinting at good breeding.

"Howdy, ma'am," Mark replied, removing his hand from the Colt's butt and wondering what brought her to the barn at such an inappropriate moment.

"I came to ask the owner to prepare Papa's buckboard," she remarked as she drew nearer. "Is he here?"

"Gone to the races, most likely," Mark answered. "I reckon most everybody's out there."

"So it seems," smiled the girl. "Aren't you going?"

"I'm waiting for somebody."

Even as he spoke, thoughts rushed into Mark's head. There he was, waiting for the possible arrival of a dangerous criminal, and he allowed a girl to come in, walk up to him like they had known each other for years. So would nine men out of ten. She looked so sweet, innocent, and harmless that any suspicions seemed stupid. Yet two men died. Skilled fighting men, one a master with a sword and the other a peace officer who took no chances when dealing with men. Both would relax if faced by such a woman as the blond.

At that moment Mark heard the sound of feet approaching the stable and a voice called, "Ina, we've done the first!"

Involuntarily Mark turned his head toward the door. Then he heard a low hiss from the blond and swung toward her. The change on the girl's face jolted Mark worse than would any male threat. Instead of the look of placid interest, her features twisted into lines of savage ecstasy such as he had never seen before, horrifying in such a setting. Already her right hand had entered the muff and emerged holding a wicked-looking, clipped-point knife of the kind once supplied as an accessory to a muzzle-loading rifle.

Even then, against a man, Mark might have drawn and shot, but his attacker being a woman froze his normally lightning-fast reactions. Sheer instinct caused him to jerk back as the knife's eight-inch blade licked toward him. He felt a burning pain between two of his ribs, his feet struck something on the floor, and he fell backward to crash his head into the side of a stall. Through the pain mists that whirled stronger and deeper, Mark heard a woman's voice. One deeper, huskier, and more seductive in tone than that of the blond.

"Two in a week, Ina," it said. "That's going some, even for you."

Then everything went black for Mark.

The two men in the county office were bored and not a little riled at being assigned to that duty when their more fortunate companions spent time among the crowds watching the various events.

"It's all 'cause I licked the marshal's neffy," stated the elderly deputy. "That's why he—"

A knock at the door interrupted his words. Exchanging glances, the deputy and the Ranger reached toward their guns. Leaving his chair, the deputy went to the window, which offered him a view of the rear door. He saw two quietly dressed women by the door, the younger supporting her companion. From their appearance, the visitors belonged to the class known as "good" women, as opposed to their sisters who worked in saloons; although the tawny-haired younger had the kind of figure best suited to a dance-hall frock.

"I'll go see what's up," the deputy stated.

"Sure," agreed the Ranger. "We don't want to rile the taxpayers."

"Or the taxpayers' wives, which's a danged sight worse," agreed the deputy.

On opening the door, he found that the girl justified his long-range judgment as far as shape and features went. Her face held an appealing expression that showed the need for a big, strong man's aid.

"My aunt's caught an attack of vapors, sir," she said, supporting the bigger woman. "Why, the town's so empty that I just didn't know where to turn for help. So I knocked on your door hoping there'd be somebody inside."

"You'd best bring her in, miss," the deputy replied. "Here, let me help. It's all right, Ranger. Just a sick lady needing a sit in the shade."

Had the deputy been more observant he would have noticed the bigger woman's right hand come from the reticule gripped in her left as he spoke.

"Th-there are more of you here?" she gasped without looking up.

"Just the two of us, ma'am," replied the deputy. "Sheriff and Ranger captain allowed somebody'd best keep guard on things here."

"How shrewd," the woman said as her companion and the deputy helped her into the room. "I do hope the banks are also protected."

"They sure as he—sure are, ma'am," the deputy assured her. "Three fellers in each and all with shotguns. Your money's safe there."

"My, isn't that a relief."

While she spoke, the woman allowed the deputy to lower her into a chair. They were in the office that contained the safe, and the woman's eyes darted toward it, then up at her companion.

"Can we do anything for you, ma'am?" asked the Ranger in concern, walking by the girl and toward the woman.

"I'm fine," she replied, her right hand slipping into the reticule that rested on her lap, coming out and driving toward the inside of the deputy's thigh.

Shock and agony passed across the old-timer's face as he felt burning pain blaze through his leg, followed by something hot and stickily wet gushing down it. Even as he tried to straighten up and draw his gun, the woman's left hand slipped from the reticule's strap and clamped hold of his throat. Such was her strength that the deputy might have been hard-pressed to resist, even without his lifeblood gushing out of the severed great saphenous vein and femoral artery.

Sudden realization hit the Ranger and his hand dipped gun-ward. Behind him, the tawny-haired girl slid a knife from her reticule and thrust savagely. Clearly she knew more than a little about using a knife, or achieved a lucky hit, for the blade drove in just right to catch the Ranger's kidneys. Unmentionable pain tore through him, numbing his limbs and choking off his cry for help. His legs buckled and he crumpled in a dying heap on the ground.

"Not bad," the big woman, whom Danny knew as Miss Cosethorpe, remarked as she wiped the knife clean on the dead deputy's shirt. "Ina's a good teacher."

"What about the other places?" asked the girl, ignoring the last comment.

"We can forget them. Three guards would be too many for us to manage. It's lucky I thought to have you knock, Tawny, or we'd've warned them. Let's take a look at that safe."

"Can you open it?" Tawny inquired after the woman crossed to and examined the safe's door.

"If the bank at Brownsville'd been this easy, you wouldn't've had to sleep with the banker and make an impression of his keys."

"I got well paid for it," sniffed the girl.

Opening her reticule, Miss Cosethorpe took out and spread open a roll of cloth to show a set of tools such as locksmiths used. Telling the girl to watch out of the window, she set to work on the safe's lock. After putting away the knife, Tawny drew a short-barreled Webley Bulldog from the reticule and held it in a competent manner while standing by the window. Ten minutes ticked by and the girl heard her companion let out a low hiss of satisfaction. Turning, Tawny saw Miss Cosethorpe pull open the safe's door. Tarrant County had never felt the need for a more modern and stronger safe, as it only rarely held much of value, and now paid the price for the negligence.

"Not as much as I hoped for," Miss Cosethorpe remarked, taking out pads of money to slip into pockets built into her skirt. "It'll cover our expenses and leave a good bit over."

"We'd best go get Ina afore she starts tossing matches around," Tawny replied, also hiding money in her skirt. "I don't know which she likes more, lighting fires or sticking a knife into somebody."

"She's got her uses," answered Miss Cosethorpe.

"Reckon that Ranger she killed told anybody about her?"

"If he had, they'd've been around asking questions before now. Lord! After all that time he still remembered her."

Ignoring the bodies of the men they murdered, the two women prepared to leave. While Miss Cosethorpe locked the empty safe, Tawny opened the door and made sure they could leave undetected. Such was the careful design of their skirts that neither gave any sign of the money she carried.

Nobody saw the two women leave and lock the office or walking through the streets to the Bayswater livery barn. On their arrival, they found the blond girl standing over Mark, and Tawny said the words he heard just before lapsing into unconsciousness.

"He's not dead," Miss Cosethorpe said, looking down at the blond giant.

"Shall I finish him off?" asked the blond girl eagerly.

"Drag him into a stall and leave him," replied the big woman calmly. "He'll bleed to death before he's found."

"How about us?" Tawny inquired.

"We'll do like we planned. Go back to the hotel and—"

"Somebody's coming!" Tawny hissed, gliding to stand by the side of the door and slipping the Webley Bulldog from her reticule.

At the same moment Miss Cosethorpe heard the sound of approaching feet and pulled a stubby Remington Double Derringer from a holster strapped to her wrist.

Walking toward the barn, Dusty Fog looked around him at the sights of the deserted town. After watching a couple of races, he had decided to relieve Mark for a time and strolled back. His eyes went to the front of the barn, through the open doors, to something that lay on the floor. With sickening impact he realized that the things were a pair of male legs clad in very familiar trousers and boots. Instantly Dusty's left hand flashed across to draw the right-side Colt and he plunged forward, ready for trouble.

As he passed through the doors of the barn, Dusty saw the beautiful blond girl and Miss Cosethorpe bending over Mark's stretched frame. With his training and serious thought on the matter, Dusty could claim to be the finest practical revolver shot and most deadly gunfighter in Texas. When he entered the barn, he came ready to shoot if necessary. But seeing women before him caused him to hesitate, even though one of them lined a Remington Double Derringer at him and the other still grasped a knife red with his friend's blood.

That hesitation gave Miss Cosethorpe her chance. The wicked little hideout gun spat out its .41-caliber load and Dusty felt a shattering impact against his stomach. Leaping forward as the small Texan doubled over, Tawny swung her Webley and crashed its gun butt against the back of his head. While the Stetson partially halted the blow, it sent him crashing down onto his face. The Colt in his hand, held cocked and with the trigger drawn back, cracked, but its bullet did no more than churn up the ground.

"Let me kill him!" purred Ina, making delicate, almost beautiful gestures with the bloody knife.

"There's no time now," Miss Cosethorpe answered. "I hit him in the guts and he's as good as gone even if Tawny hadn't split his head. Somebody might have heard the shot. Let's get the hell out of here!"

For some time after the women left, Dusty lay doubled over in agony on the floor. Then, slowly, he dragged himself to his knees. Face twisted in the pain that knotted his guts and sent waves of hideous nausea through him, he dragged himself up by gripping the side of the door. For a moment Dusty thought he would collapse, but forced himself to stay erect. From the region of the pain, he guessed that the bullet must have caught him in the belly and knew that both he and Mark must receive medical aid in a hurry. Leaning against the door, Dusty managed to draw his right-hand Colt, the other lying on the ground where he let it fall. Although every move caused him untold torment and agony, he gripped the Colt in his right hand and forced back the trigger as his left swung across to knock back the hammer. Using the method known as fanning, Dusty fired off three shots.

Everything seemed to be whirling around, the ground heaving underfoot as if stuck by an earthquake. Dusty wanted nothing more than to double over and sink to the ground, but he forced himself to continue standing. In the distance voices raised as men, attracted by the sound of the shots, tried to locate their source. With an effort Dusty managed to force back the Colt's hammer, and another shot rang out. Then he sank down, unable to prevent himself from vomiting and finding mists swirling before his eyes.

Feet thudded, drawing closer, yet very slowly it seemed to Dusty. He fought to stay conscious, wanting to warn the men of their danger. At last the entire Bad Bunch business came through as clear as daylight. So simple—and yet the last thing any man would think of.

Approaching cautiously, one man from each of the banks appeared on the scene. Behind them, the other guards stood gripping shotguns in locked buildings, in case the shots should be a means of luring part of the various banks' defenses away before a robbery attempt.

"Cap'n Fog!" gasped one of Murat's Rangers, dropping to his knees and thrusting away his Colt.

"In-Inside!" Dusty croaked, every word tearing pain through him. "M-Mark's there!"

"Who did it?" asked the man, while his companions dashed into the barn.

"Wo . . . wo . . . !" Desperately Dusty tried to give his warning. A sudden surge of pain tore through him, the mists swirled thicker, and he collapsed unconscious.

"Get a hoss out!" the Ranger yelled. "Ride like hell for a doctor, there's one at the hoss races."

While one man obeyed, the other went to the rear door of the barn and looked out. He saw no sign of the two Texans' attackers and the ground was too hard to show tracks. Turning, he joined the Ranger.

"Lord!" the man breathed. "I'd hate like hell to tangle with the jaspers who could do this to Dusty Fog and Mark Counter."

13

THE WOMAN'S TOUCH

Although a small lamp threw out a feeble glow on the table by the window, the bed lay in comparative darkness. Opening his eyes, Dusty tried to sit up and gave a low groan as the pain tore through his lower body. Betty Hardin rose from where she had sat for the past hour and crossed to the bed. Typically, Dusty's first thought went to his *amigo*.

"How . . . how's Mark?" he asked.

"He's alive," the girl answered. "Badly cut, but only the flesh between the ribs. Lon thinks he must have been pulling back as whoever did it cut, and the knife didn't go right in."

"Thank God for that!" Dusty breathed. "How about me?"

Each word took an effort, for his head throbbed and his raised hand told him that bandages covered the top of his skull. Walking to the side table, Betty picked up Dusty's gun belt and brought it to the bed.

"You're the luckiest cuss alive, Dusty," she told him, holding the belt out. "The bullet hit the buckle and doubled you over."

Studying the almost doubled condition of the stout buckle, Dusty felt as if a cold hand touched him. An inch higher, or lower, and the bullet would have torn into his body. As it was, the .41 bullet caught the buckle and slammed it into his midsection with the power of a mule kick.

"It sure made a mess of that," Dusty said, trying to sound better than he felt.

"Somebody tried to make a mess of your pumpkin head," snorted Betty. "If you hadn't been wearing your hat—"

"Maw always tried to teach Danny and me to take our hats off around women," Dusty interrupted. "I never learned."

"What's that mean?"

"The Bad Bunch are women."

"Now you take it easy, Dusty boy. Your head's not broken, but it still caught one hell of a crack."

"Damn it, Betty!" Dusty barked, trying to sit up. "I tell you it was women who did this—"

Gently Betty placed her hands on Dusty's shoulders and he felt too weak to struggle against her. So he lay back on the pillow and the girl nodded her head.

"That's better. I'll go tell Belle and Lon you've woken up."

"Is Jules here?"

"No. He's down at the county offices. They were robbed and the two guards killed. Take it easy, Dusty. I won't be long."

Watching Betty leave the room, Dusty put a hand on his stomach and winced. Women! He should have thought of that possibility and had even less excuse for not doing so with a girl like Belle Boyd around to remind him of just how dangerous a member of the "weaker" sex could be.

Everything fell into place. Beau Amesley, a southern gentleman of the old school, would never allow a man other than one he knew and trusted approach him under the conditions he faced that night in Brownsville; but seeing that pretty, well-dressed blond girl, he suspected nothing until too late. Much the same applied to Prince. While he would be ready to throw down on a man, such a beautiful girl . . .

"A face like an angel!"

As the words from so long ago came back to him, Dusty jerked up in bed. The movement drove nausea through him to lie back again until the spasm passed. To take his mind off the pain, he tried to think.

Could the blond possibly be the girl abducted from the massacred Quaker village at the end of the war? It hardly seemed likely—yet she had an innocent, almost angelic beauty. Maybe she only looked like the Quaker girl. Yet if Prince saw her, he could have left his work following McKie and gone after her. With his normal alertness relaxed, he would prove easy meat, although no *man* would have found him so.

"Where're my clothes?" he asked as Betty appeared, followed by the Kid and Belle. "I've got to . . ."

"They're in the cupboard—and staying there," Betty answered.

"Damn it, Betty, I have to see Jules—"

"You lie back and do like Betty says," ordered the Kid. "Do it, Dusty, or, so help me, I'll hawg-tie you down. And you're weak enough for me to be able to do it, even if the gals don't help."

"Which we will," warned Belle. "You'll be neither use nor ornament in your condition, Dusty."

More than the threat, a wave of dizziness caused Dusty to lie back. When it passed, he looked at his cousin and friends.

"That's better," Betty smiled. "First time I ever saw any of you floating outfit yahoos show good sense."

"I treats that remark with the contempt it deserves," growled the Kid. "Now, Dusty, what's up?"

"Who shot you, Dusty, is what he means," Belle went on.

"A woman—"

"That figures," the Kid said. "I didn't reckon any man could."

"I know this sounds crazy," Dusty continued, ignoring the comment. "But I reckon the Bad Bunch are something to do with Hannah's guerrillas."

"You mean that bunch Company C wiped out in the war?" asked Betty. "But you killed them all."

"All the men, sure. But not the women. Last I saw of them, the Yankees were taking them off for their provost marshal to handle."

"What happened to them?" Belle inquired.

"I don't know. As soon as I came in, Uncle Devil sent me off with Cousin Red and Billy Jack to warn our folks the war had ended."

"Then why . . . ?" Betty began.

"The woman who shot me was the big one Hannah sent out to dicker with us. She escaped. I tell you, Betty gal, she was one you'd never forget."

"Do you think a guerrilla's camp follower would have the brains for something like the Bad Bunch's robberies, Dusty?" Belle said.

"Hannah figured she was smart enough to come out and learn just how dangerous the situation was," Dusty replied. "And she sure as hell wasn't kept for her good looks. I reckon she'd be smart enough."

"What did she look like, Dusty?" asked Belle, and after he described the woman went on, "She shouldn't be hard to find, even with all the strangers in town. Let's go, Lon."

Betty looked down at her cousin, then went to draw the right-hand Colt from his holster. "I'll borrow this, Cousin Dusty."

"Why?" he asked.

"If we find her, I don't think she'll come easy."

"We can handle her, Betty," Belle stated.

"Dusty's my cousin and Mark's been a real good friend," Betty replied. "Besides, there are three of them at least from what Dusty says."

"I only saw two," admitted Dusty, and raised a hand to his bandaged head. "But neither of them could have hit me."

"Reckon I need help, Betty gal?" asked the Kid, his face Comanche mean in the lamp's light.

"Against men, no," answered Betty. "But you're going after three women."

"Betty's right, Lon," Belle went on. "A lot of men have died because they hesitated before throwing down on a woman. Let's go."

Without any more argument, the Kid followed the girls from the room. Dusty realized that he could do nothing in his present state. So he lay back and closed his eyes, drifting off to sleep.

Midnight chimed on the clock in the hall as Betty and the Kid entered Dusty's room. The small Texan opened his eyes and they crossed to the bed.

"We found out where two of them stayed," Betty told Dusty. "But they've pulled out."

"Likely left town," the Kid went on. "And no damned chance of finding their sign afore morning."

"Where's Belle to?"

"She's off with Jules, said she had things to do."

Not until noon the following day did Dusty learn of the "things" that kept Belle and Jules Murat busy all night. To say the least, her doings handed Dusty quite a shock. Coming into the room, Belle held out a copy of the *Fort Worth Herald*. Although it was Sunday, the *Herald*'s editor considered the events of the previous day rated bringing out his paper. Its headlines blazed before Dusty's eyes: "DUSTY FOG, MARK COUNTER, TWO PEACE OFFICERS KILLED IN DARING DAYLIGHT ROBBERY."

"What the . . . ?" Dusty gasped and snatched the paper from the girl's hands to read how he and Mark had been found dead in the livery barn. He read no more but glared at Belle. "Damn it, word'll spread about this. If Mark and my folks—"

"Jules and I sent telegraph messages to the Rio Hondo and Mark's father," Belle replied. "They'll know you're alive. The Bad Bunch won't. We had to make the women think you died without talking and that their secret's still safe. Otherwise they might just keep going out of Texas and be lost to us."

"Reckon they won't as it is?"

"Why should they? As far as they know, nobody suspects them. They've a good organization and safe hideout someplace. I reckon they'll stick. I'll be pulling out on tomorrow's stage."

"Why?"

"To find them," Belle said quietly. "This chore needs a woman's touch."

"I'll be on my feet in a few days . . ." Dusty began, but the girl shook her head. "Then take Lon."

"This's a *woman's* chore, Dusty," Belle said gently. "No man can get near the Bad Bunch."

"If there's anything we can do—"

"Betty knows what I want. There're a few details to tie together, but we've worked the main idea out. Now I want to talk to Mark."

"How is the stubborn ole cuss?"

"Sore, weak, and hungry. I'll see you before I leave, Dusty."

As Dusty predicted, the story of the robbery spread across the range country. Many newspapers in other states and territories carried the news of his and Mark's death. In the Indian nations a girl read it, her shoulders shaking with silent sobs. Up at a railroad construction camp, another girl heard the news and cursed bitterly, savagely, with great breadth of expression as tears poured down her freckled cheeks. After the first signs of grief passed, each girl collected certain items and took separate ways toward Texas.

For almost two months Belle Boyd lived as a saloon girl in the hope of finding a member of the Bad Bunch. Guessing that Miss Cosethorpe kept girls in the bigger towns to scout for likely prospects, Belle began her quest in Galveston. Aided by the U.S. Secret Service— General Handiman owed Dusty Fog too great a favor to raise objections, even if he wished to do so—Belle learned which saloon was most frequented by bankers and big businessmen. She worked there for two weeks, while the town prepared to celebrate a naval festival. It came and went, but the Bad Bunch failed to make an appearance.

San Antone seemed the next likely place, offering a county fair of some size, and there Belle made her way. Every day she expected to hear a retraction of the story concerning Dusty's and Mark's death, but it never came. Slipping out of Fort Worth one night, they returned to the Rio Hondo and stayed out of the public's eye on the OD Connected.

Arriving early at San Antone, Belle easily found a place in the best saloon. Expecting a rush of business, the owner hired a girl of Belle's looks without hesitation. During the next ten days Belle wondered if she might be in the wrong place, but visiting other saloons produced no likely candidate for the Bad Bunch's scout. Then a new girl came to the Gallant Defenders Saloon and Belle felt sure that pay dirt had been struck.

Mitzi Zorko had brunette hair, a pretty face, and a plump but shapely figure of the kind highly regarded at that time. On the surface, little separated her from the other regular saloon employees. However, Belle noticed that Mitzi's skin bore a tan rarely seen among saloon girls, and that she had muscular legs and arms. Not much to go on, but enough taken with the jewelry she wore. While a saloon girl always wore trinkets of some kind, diamonds were not a standard item. The ring, bracelet, and earrings sported by Mitzi all carried genuine stones.

Being skilled in her work, Belle watched for two days before feeling certain. Mitzi made no friends among the other girls, but showed attention toward the president of the town's largest bank. Satisfied that she had found what she wanted, Belle contacted one of the Rangers, who had followed her on her travels. With him ready to play his part, Belle put her plan into operation.

Slipping away from the group of cowhands she had been helping to entertain, Belle followed Mitzi through the rear door of the barroom and across the walled-in yard to the women's backhouse. Night had fallen and the town boomed with noisy life. Although she did not show it, Belle entered the backhouse ready to put her extensive knowledge of savate into use if needed. Mitzi glanced at Belle and opened her mouth to make some comment.

"You've got trouble, Mitzi," Belle said before the other could speak. "The Texas Rangers know you work for the Bad Bunch."

For a plump girl Mitzi could move fast. Lunging past Belle, she put her back to the door, then fetched a push dagger from its garter sheath. From the way she held it, Mitzi knew how to handle the wicked little knife.

"What did you say!" she hissed.

"Hey now!" Belle yapped. "Quit that, I'm on your side. It's just that when I saw that Ranger watching, I figured he was after me. But I followed him and heard him talking to one of the deputies."

"Why'd he be after you?"

"Because I'm Belle Starr."

"Be-Belle Starr?"

"That's what I said," Belle answered, right hand dipping into her reticule to produce a Remington Double

Derringer and line it at the other girl's belly. "Put the prat cutter away, Mitzi, we're both in the same game."

That would be true enough, had Belle been the girl she claimed; except that Belle Starr never employed violence in the commission of a crime. Clearly Mitzi felt impressed by Belle's assumed identity. Using the outlaw's term for a small hideout knife strengthened the impression that Belle belonged to the criminal element, as did the way she produced the Remington.

"How'd you get onto me?" Mitzi asked, sliding away the push dagger.

"Easy, no ordinary calico cat could afford to wear real blazers like those," Belle replied, indicating the ring and bracelet. "Maybe the Ranger got onto you the same way—unless somebody told him."

"Who'd tell him?" demanded Mitzi; then a scowl creased her face. "Unless it was that cow Georgie up in Wichita Falls. I licked her good last time we met at the spread."

"Thing being, what're we going to do," Belle put in.

"We?"

"Why not? I've always wanted to tie in with a smart bunch of women owlhoots, and this's my chance."

"How'd you know we're all women?" asked Mitzi suspiciously.

"I figured it out," Belle replied. "No man could have got into that guarded office in Fort Worth. I know two who went down to try, and called it off when they saw the guards. But the guards'd open the door for women."

"Smart thinking."

"Let's get moving. I've a notion your boss might find interesting."

Apparently Belle satisfied Mitzi as to her bona fides, for the brunette nodded and opened the door. Then shut it again, fast.

"There's a feller with a law badge out by the saloon door!" she whispered.

"Let me look," Belle answered, and pulled the door open slightly. "It's the Ranger. Give me your knife."

"I can han—"

"He'll not give *you* a chance, but he doesn't know me," Belle interrupted.

Seeing the wisdom of Belle's words, Mitzi handed over her push dagger and listened to what the other girl told her. Then Belle opened the door and walked across the yard.

"Hey, handsome," she greeted the Ranger. "You-all looking for li'l ole me?"

"Nope," he replied, and nodded to where Mitzi stepped out of the backhouse. "For her."

With that he walked by Belle and toward Mitzi. Steel glinted in Belle's hand and she lunged at the man's back. Mitzi saw Belle strike, heard the Ranger gasp as his back arched in what appeared to be a mortal pain, then he went down. After wiping the push dagger's blade on the man's shirt, Belle walked over to where Mitzi stood open mouthed and staring.

"Is he . . . ?" Mitzi gasped, for she had never been on an actual robbery or seen sudden death.

"Dead as a six-day, stunk-up skunk," Belle answered, offering her the knife. "Now let's get moving."

Showing no inclination to make a closer examination of the Ranger, Mitzi took and sheathed the dagger. Then she followed Belle to the rear gate and they went out through it. After the gate closed, the Ranger looked up carefully. He rose to his feet, dusted off his clothes, and grinned broadly.

"Sid," he told himself with satisfaction. "You-all should be in the theater. That chubby li'l gal thinks you're dead for certain sure."

Having given himself justifiable praise, the Ranger ambled off to the rear gate, waited for a time to let Belle get well clear, then went to complete his part in the plan.

After collecting their property from the small hotel which housed most of the Gallant Defenders' girls, Belle and Mitzi went across the town. Clearly Mitzi followed a prearranged plan, for she led the way to a street that formed part of the Houston trail. Waving down a stagecoach, which took advantage of a full moon to cover some miles in comparatively cool conditions, she paid their fares to a way station sixty miles from San Antone. The driver had often picked up saloon girls making a hurried departure from towns and asked no questions. Only one passenger rode the coach, an old man already asleep, but the girls talked little and said nothing at all that might arouse his suspicions.

Leaving the stage at the way station, ostensibly to await a southbound connection, Belle found that she could not inform her friends of her location. At first she hoped either to telegraph Murat or leave a message for him, but she realized that would be impossible. From all signs, the woman who owned the way station either belonged to, or worked for, the Bad Bunch. As soon as the coach disappeared, she sent her Mexican staff to check stores in the cellar and saddled two good horses. Supplying men's clothing, the woman told the girls to change, and as they prepared to leave whispered something to Mitzi.

"Can we trust her?" Belle asked as they rode off to the northwest.

"Sure. The boss put her into that way station. If the law comes and asks, she'll say we stole two horses and rode off to the east."

"Your boss's real smart," Belle commented.

"She sure is. Got gals scattered all over the state, so that any of us who has anything to pass on can do it. Mae back there told me where to meet the boss."

"Can you find the place?" asked Belle.

"Sure I can. The boss trained us real good."

"How'd she learn all these things?"

"Back in the war she ran a band of guerrillas. The Texas Light Cavalry wiped the band out, but Anna got away herself and saved all her gals, too."

"Anna!" Belle breathed.

"Anna Gould, the boss," Mitzi explained.

Belle did not reply, but thoughts churned in her head. It seemed that Dusty called the play right. Yet he lacked one detail. The big woman had not merely been "something to do with Hannah's guerrillas," she was their leader. While everybody assumed "Hannah" to be the name of the band's male leader, it had been commanded by a woman called Anna Gould.

14

TOO MANY BELLE STARRS

"So you're Belle Starr, huh?" Anna Gould said, looking Belle Boyd over from head to foot. "That's strange."

After riding for four days, making good time, and living off food supplied by the woman at the way station, the girls had just arrived at the Bad Bunch's hideout. Built originally by wild horse hunters, the camp consisted of a large cabin and a pole corral set halfway along the bottom of a pleasant, if steep-sided, valley close to the Ronde River.

During the ride, Belle learned much about the Bad Bunch by pumping her companion. Mitzi needed little pumping, being naturally garrulous in safe company. So Belle came into information that might be of use and also found out the answers to a few things that would certainly interest Dusty Fog. Nothing Belle heard about the Bad Bunch's leader led her to assume that she faced a simple task now that the gang had been located. From her first sight of Anna Gould and the Bad Bunch, Belle knew for sure her assumption had been correct.

Behind Anna, dressed in men's shirts and denim pants, stood her two invariable companions. Looking as sensually attractive as one woman possibly could in her snug-fitting clothes, Tawny eyed Belle with mocking gaze. At her left, Ina toyed with the handle of the sheathed knife and still managed to retain her air of angelic innocence. A further pair of girls came from the cabin, a slim redhead and a beautiful blond. The latter caught Belle's eye as she advanced, for her face showed intelligence and refinement. In the overlarge men's clothing, the blond's figure did not show to good advantage, but Belle judged she would be every bit as voluptuous as Tawny given a chance.

"What's strange about it?" Belle asked, looking back to Anna Gould.

"Dora rode in last night," Tawny answered for her boss. "And guess who she brought with her."

"Who?" demanded Mitzi, although Belle began to feel that *she* could supply the answer.

"According to Dora," purred Tawny. "She brought in Belle Starr, too."

Which confirmed the thoughts Belle had formed on the matter. For all that, she acted just as the genuine Belle Starr might when faced with an impostor.

"Where is she?" Belle spat out. "I'll show you who's—"

"Hey, Belle," called Tawny, turning toward the blond. "Come on up and get acquainted with Belle Starr."

Surprise and anger flashed across the blond's face. "Is this a joke?"

"If it is, girlie," Belle spat out. "I'm not laughing."

"Nor are we—girlie," warned Anna Gould.

Watched by the other women, Belle and the blond faced each other as tense and alert as two bobcats meeting on a narrow ledge. Suddenly Ina stared off into the distance and pointed.

"Two riders," she said.

The girl had keen eyes, for when Belle followed the

direction Ina pointed, she could see no more than a pair of distant dots. However, Anna appeared fully satisfied with Ina's sight powers.

"Push those pair into the cabin until we know who it is, Tawny!" Anna ordered. "If I find there's . . ."

Letting the words trail off, Anna swung back to study the riders. Tawny jerked a thumb toward the cabin and the other girls hovered around menacingly. Realizing that the time had not come to make her move, Belle obeyed without argument. The blond eyed Belle appraisingly, and with menace flickering in her eyes, followed on her heels. Throwing open the door, Tawny stood aside.

"While you're in there, decide which of you's Belle Starr," she told them. "And Lord help the one who isn't."

After Belle and the blond entered the cabin, Tawny slammed and locked its door. Even before Belle could speak, the blond caught her by the arm and heaved her across the single room. No matter who she might be, the blond had strength. Belle shot forward and only just managed to turn before hitting the wall.

"I don't know who you are, or what your game is," the blond stated, moving forward. "But by the time I'm done with you, you'll wish you'd never used my name."

Watching the blond, Belle noticed how she advanced with clenched fists and in the manner of one well versed in the business of self-defense. Unless Belle called the play wrong, the other girl could give her a hell of a fight, one which might incapacitate them both at a time when each needed to be fully fit and mobile.

The cabin offered room to maneuver, being scantily furnished. Despite the money their raids brought in, the Bad Bunch made do with a table, four chairs, a couple of cupboards, a kitchen stove, and a dozen bunks. Female and male clothes were scattered about the room, and a couple of rifles and shotguns stood on a wall rack to complete the furnishings.

Avoiding the blond's advance, Belle darted across to look out the window. All the four girls stood with Anna some distance away from the cabin and watching the approaching riders. Just in time, she turned to meet the advancing blond.

"Mark Counter is alive!" Belle said hurriedly.

The blond came to a halt as if she had run into an invisible wall.

"Wh-what did you say?" she gasped.

"He was knifed in the robbery, but he's still alive. The newspaper story was a lie."

Various emotions played on the blond's face and she seemed dazed by the news. "If this's a trick . . ." she began.

"No more than the night you played cards with him in your room at the hotel in Elkhorn*," Belle replied and tensed slightly. "What hands did you both hold?"

If the blond failed to give the right answer, Belle meant to launch a savate attack. With her own life at stake, she did not aim to take chances.

"We each held a royal flush," the blond said, sounding dazed. "You're not lying about Mark being alive?"

"The last time I saw him, he was finishing a chicken," Belle smiled. "He told me about the card game and other things."

"Who are you?" asked the blond.

"Belle Boyd."

"The rebel spy!"

"That's what they called me. And you're Belle Starr."

"I'm Belle Starr," admitted the blond. "Mark—alive!"

"Which's more than we'll be unless we come up with some answers," Belle commented. "I think it's best that we try to make them think neither of us is you."

* Told in *Troubled Range*.

"It could be," Belle Starr agreed. "But how do we do that?"

"They know that you can take care of yourself in a fight. So let's make them think neither of us can fight and they might accept that we both pretended to be you."

"And then?"

"We'll have to think up some story for wanting to join them."

"They're still watching those riders," Belle Starr said, glancing from the window. "We can each claim we thought that the Bad Bunch would take us if they thought we were the notorious Belle Starr."

"Can you fix a reason for wanting to join them?" Belle Boyd asked. "I've got it arranged that I was Betty Hardin's maid and fired for stealing."

"And I worked in my uncle's bank in Newton, as a come-on to draw in depositors," Belle Starr went on. "Only I got tired of it and lit out with some of the bank's money and a set of duplicate keys."

"Can you prove it?"

"I can raise money and a set of convincing keys."

"Let's hope it doesn't come to that," Belle Boyd said. "Let's hope she goes for my idea first. If she does, we'll nail her hide to the wall—"

"Or be dead ourselves," Belle Starr answered. "She plays rough and for keeps. Which of them knifed Mark?"

"The blond."

"Then she's mine when the time comes," Belle Starr gritted. "I'll—"

"That tawny-haired bitch's coming back," warned Belle Boyd. "Let's make it look good." She raised her voice. "Why, you cheap blond cow, I'll snatch you bald headed for sure!"

"You just try it, you scraggy whore!" Belle Starr screeched back.

"Whore!" Belle Boyd howled. "Why, you!"

With that, as the door opened, she threw herself at the blond and they tangled in the most amateurish manner they could manage. Hands dug into hair, although not pulling, the two Belles staggered, spun around, and headed for the door. If their plan was to succeed, they must put on their show before all the Bad Bunch and not just for Tawny's benefit. Leaping aside, Tawny allowed the girls to pass her. Their squeals and sudden appearance drew the attention of all the party outside, including that of the two new arrivals. Neither of the Belles noticed the newcomers as they sprawled to the ground or rolled over and over, flailing wildly at each other. While the black-haired, good-looking, and shapely new arrival appeared to be a member of the Bad Bunch, the other would have interested Belle Starr.

An expensive black Stetson sat back on a mop of short, curly hair. Beneath it, a tanned, freckled, good-looking face bore an expression of reckless zest for life. She wore a man's shirt and denim pants that looked as if they had been bought a size too small and shrunk in washing, clinging to and emphasizing her full bust, trim waist, and richly curved hips. At five foot seven, she did not quite equal Tawny's height, but showed just as good a figure and wore an outfit designed to see it off to its best advantage. From her moccasin-covered feet to the top of her hat, the redhead gave an impression of hardy, tough self-reliance and her arms, bare to above the elbow, carried strong muscles.

A puzzled expression flickered over the redhead's face as she stared at Belle Starr, but went fast. Before Anna could turn and see the newcomer's interest in the blond, her chance passed.

"Is this the best your gals can manage in a fight?" asked the redhead, nodding contemptuously at the struggling pair.

An angry snort broke from Tawny, but Anna silenced her with a glare. "They aren't in my gang. Fact being, they both claim to be Belle Starr, too."

"You're saying that pair of cathouse culls came here claiming to be me?" yelled the redhead.

With that she stormed forward to where the two Belles sat gasping as if exhausted and exchanged weak slaps or hairtugs. The blond stared at the redhead, opening her mouth as if to speak. Down scooped the redhead's hands, sinking into each girl's hair. She jerked the two heads apart and brought them forward again, propelling one against the other hard. Even as Belle Boyd realized her danger, she felt the redhead slow her head down. It still collided with Belle Starr's, but with far less force than appeared to the watchers. Releasing the dazed girls' hair, the redhead allowed them to collapse to the ground.

"You reckon either of 'em's me?" she demanded, swinging to face Anna.

"I always heard Belle Starr was a mighty tough girl," Anna admitted. "And good with a gun, too."

"Happen you tell Carrie here to bring my gun belt from her hoss, I'll easy answer that for you."

"Go ahead, Carrie," Anna ordered the black-haired new arrival. "I don't reckon you'll object to us taking the percussion caps off the nipples before you start— Belle?"

"Don't you trust me?" asked the redhead.

"Let's say I'm just careful."

"I always did like working with careful folks."

Carrie went to where a fine-looking buckskin gelding and a roan stood by the corral. Taking the gun belt from the roan's saddle, she returned and handed it to Anna. After Anna had removed the caps from the ivory-handled Navy Colt, she put it back into the contoured twist-hand draw holster and passed the belt to the redhead. From the swift, practiced way she strapped on the belt,

the redhead had worn it regularly. Nor did she show
any of the slightly self-conscious attitude all but Tawny
of the Bad Bunch presented when wearing their gun
belts.

Facing the others, apart from the still-dazed pair lying behind her, the redhead suddenly twisted her right
hand palm out, curled fingers around the Colt's butt,
and slid it smoothly from the holster. While drawing,
she thumbed back the hammer and depressed the trigger with her forefinger. A concerted gasp rose from the
watching women as the Colt, cocked and ready to fire,
lined on Anna's middle a bare second after the hand's
first movement.

Maybe a one-second draw could not compare with
the speed of a real fast man, but it exceeded anything
even Tawny of the Bad Bunch had achieved. Cold anger, mingled with a touch of worry, clouded Tawny's
face as she watched the redhead continue to display a
spectacular ability at fancy gun handling. Around
pinwheeled the Colt, first forward and then to the rear.
Next the redhead tossed it into the air to make it turn
over and land butt-first in her hand once more. After
other fancy moves, she showed the border shift: tossing
the Colt from her right hand to the left in the manner of
experts in the *pistolero* arts. To admiring exclamations,
she finished off by twirling the gun, twisting it, and
catching it around the cylinder, then slipped it back
into leather.

While the display went on, none of the Bad Bunch
had eyes for the two dazed girls. Groaning a little, Belle
Boyd put a hand on her forehead. Anger roared
through her and she started to force herself up. Instantly Belle Starr caught her by the arm.

"No, Belle!" the blond whispered. "That's Calamity
Jane and she's here, like me, after the bitch who knifed
Mark."

Although Belle Boyd had never met Calamity Jane,

she knew of the other through highly colored stories that appeared in the *Police Gazette* and its contemporary magazines, also from more factual mentions by Mark Counter or Betty Hardin.* Certainly Calamity gave the impression of being tough and capable. Furthermore, despite the treatment received at the other's hands, Belle Starr clearly regarded Calamity as a friend. So Belle stayed on her hands and knees, copying the blond's dazed attitude.

At the conclusion of her show, Calamity unbuckled the belt and passed it to Carrie. Fury showed on Tawny's face as the other girls gathered around the redhead and passed favorable comments on what they had just witnessed. Calamity pushed by the girls and stalked to where the two Belles waited.

"All right!" she growled. "Up!"

"Ye-yes . . . ma'am . . . !" sniffed Belle Starr, rising slowly.

As she also scrambled up, Belle Boyd wondered how she might let Calamity know she was a friend. She did not need to worry. Having personal experience of Belle Starr's fighting skill, Calamity realized that the blond ought to have shown to better advantage than witnessed on her arrival. So, as Belle Starr had been softpedaling, the other girl must be a friend—or at least working in conjunction with the blond.

"So you pair of two-bit sluts reckon you're me?" Calamity hissed.

"I'm not sure that you're any more Belle Starr than they are."

Slowly Calamity turned and looked at the speaker. Tawny had come to the front of the others and Anna stood holding the Webley Bulldog revolver until recently thrust into the girl's waistband. Tense expec-

---

* Calamity Jane's story is told in *Trouble Trail, The Cow Thieves, The Big Hunt,* etc.

tancy showed on the faces of the other girls as they watched Tawny approach Calamity.

"You're not, huh?" sniffed Calamity. "As if it matters to me what the hired help thinks."

No other girl had ever dared to address Tawny in such a manner. As Anna's second in command, she ran the gang with a despotic hand and expected to assume the boss's shoes in the course of time. Yet she sensed a menace in Calamity's presence. All too well she knew that she could not equal the other's prowess with a gun, especially when using the Webley, as it lacked the Colt's superb balance and handling qualities. However, she figured to have enough of a size-weight advantage to take the redheaded interloper.

Like a flash Tawny drove her right fist around in a roundhouse punch, which smashed into Calamity's cheek and flung her backward. As the redhead's rump hit the ground, Tawny charged forward and lashed out a kick aimed at her body. If it landed, the kick might have ended the fight, but it did not land. Out stabbed Calamity's hands, catching Tawny's foot before it arrived. Then, with a twisting heave, Calamity threw Tawny off balance and tumbled her to the ground.

"Go get her, Belle!" Carrie screeched. "Stomp her good."

Needing no encouragement, Calamity flung herself forward and landed on Tawny to bear the girl down once more. Fingers sank into hair and Tawny twisted Calamity from the top, gaining the upper position for a moment. Just like the two Belles, Tawny and Calamity rolled over and over, but with one difference. Where the former pair did not try to hurt each other, the latter pair went at it with all the full, raw fury of a pair of enraged bobcats. Hard fists lashed out, striking savagely at any available part of the other girl's body. Caught in the bust by one blow, Calamity lost her upper place and went onto her back. Tawny lurched on top, kneeling astride Calamity's body and clamping fingers on her throat. Then the tawny-haired girl raised Calamity's head and shoulders, crashing them down again.

Pain ripped through Calamity and she tried to throw Tawny off. Failing, she brought up her left leg, curling it before the other's body and striking back. The hard muscles of Calamity's calf hurt Tawny, but did not dislodge her. Still her fingers clenched on the redhead's windpipe and cut off breath from her lungs. In desperation Calamity raked the sole of her moccasin across Tawny's face with such force that she crushed the girl's nose. Twice Calamity sent her foot across Tawny's face and blood ran from the other's nostrils. Pain made Tawny rear back and Calamity pitched her over. In landing, Tawny lay between Calamity's legs and the redhead closed them in a scissor hold around her middle. Now it was Tawny's turn to suffer, and the constriction of Calamity's muscles, hardened by riding and work, sent agony into the trapped torso.

"Shall we jump them now?" Belle Starr hissed to Belle Boyd, for the Bad Bunch had eyes only for the fight.

Only for a moment was Belle Boyd tempted, then cold reason held her in check and she shook her head. "No. They'd be too many for us."

In her attempts to escape from Calamity's crushing legs, Tawny got her feet on the ground and forced herself upright. She had her back to Calamity and could not turn to use fists or grabbing fingers as a means of escaping. Before Tawny made a move, Calamity rocked backward, raised the other's feet from the ground and brought her crashing down rump first. A wail of agony broke from Tawny as she struck the ground. At first she tried to force Calamity's crossed ankles apart, then, as Calamity dug fingers into her hair and tried to drag her back into position for another of those spine-shattering smashes, dragged off the redhead's left moccasin. Al-

though the move had been involuntary, Tawny saw a
chance of escape. Grasping Calamity's big toe, she
twisted at it and bent it back. Calamity screeched and
jerked her legs apart, sending her right back and then
forward to drive into the other girl's spine. Freed from
the legs, Tawny pitched forward and rolled away.

For all that, the bigger girl made her feet almost as
quickly as Calamity. As the redhead rushed, Tawny
swung a fist to catch her in the mouth. Clearly Tawny
did not intend to get too close, for she halted and started
to throw punches or slaps with desperate abandon.
While trying to move in, Calamity also lashed out with
her hands.

For ten minutes the other women stood watching a
fight to remember. Even Belle Starr, with cause to
know Calamity's ability in that line, felt awe as she
witnessed the fury of the two girls. Yet slowly it seemed
that Calamity gained the upper hand. Tawny changed
tactics first, unable to take more of Calamity's battering,
savaging fists. With hands driving into hair, she closed
and drove up her knee. Only just in time Calamity
twisted and took the impact on her thigh. Then she
threw Tawny over her hip and went down on top of the
girl.

Once more they churned around on the ground,
screaming, gasping, all but insensible to pain and wanting only to hurt the other. Again it became clear that
Tawny had met her match, but she refused to give in or
try to escape. The pace could not be maintained and
they rolled apart. Slowly, painfully, they dragged themselves erect and Calamity started to stagger forward.
Fear bit into Tawny at the sight. Sobbing, she lowered
her head and tried to butt the other girl in the stomach.
Instead Tawny stumbled and her head passed between
Calamity's spread-apart legs. Closing her legs, Calamity
trapped Tawny's head between her knees. Then she
bent forward and wrapped her arms around the girl's

thighs from above. As Tawny made a despairing effort to escape, Calamity fell backward. Tawny's head drove onto the ground with brutal force, but fortunately the springy crash cushioned some of the impact. The force of her landing tore her free and she flopped to the earth, rolling onto her back.

Sitting close by, mouth trailing open, breasts heaving, face bloody, and body mottled with bruises, Calamity knew she need do no more. An awed silence fell on the Bad Bunch as they realized their toughest member was defeated.

"Get 'em inside the cabin," Anna ordered. "Then I've questions to ask."

15

MISS BOYD
ARRANGES A CRIME

"So I thought you'd take me if you thought I was Belle Starr," finished Belle Starr after telling Anna Gould the story arranged with Belle Boyd earlier.

After helping the two battered girls into the cabin and attending to their injuries, both Belles found themselves faced with Anna Gould and demands to be told why they wanted to become members of the Bad Bunch. On the bed assigned to her, Calamity watched Belle Starr with as much approval as a multitude of bruises, lumps, and minor abrasions allowed, feeling sure the big woman believed the story.

According to Belle Starr, she had been drunk and boasting of her identity when Dora took her from the saloon in the Texas Panhandle country. Having been the drunken one, Dora went along with the story.

"Now you!" Anna ordered, looking at Belle Boyd.

Quickly Belle went through her story of being Betty Hardin's maid, dismissed for theft and the "lucky" chance of overhearing the Ranger's conversation. Once again Anna appeared to believe the story. In fact she wanted to believe it, not caring to admit even to herself that somebody might have cracked the secrecy of her organization.

Slowly levering herself into a sitting position as Belle finished, Calamity looked at Anna. "You still reckon that I'm not Belle Starr?"

"Tawny did," Anna pointed out.

Nodding to where the girl lay groaning and with face to the wall on a bed across the room, Calamity grinned. "You want for me to go over and ask if she still feels the same way?"

"No. I reckon you're Belle Starr, all right," Anna replied. "How did you get onto us?"

"Got to wondering who could take Dusty Fog and Mark Counter and knew no men could. That only left women. After that it as easy, a few questions in the right places and I found Carrie."

With her wide outlaw connections, Belle Starr just might learn enough to set her on the right track, Anna decided. Again she hated to believe that the other could fool her and so accepted Calamity's story. Her eyes went to Belle Boyd once more and she wondered if the girl might help with the next job planned for the Bad Bunch.

"So you stole Betty Hardin's jewel case," she said.

"Yes, boss, but they're nothing to what we could get down there."

"How'd you mean?"

"It'll soon be the Rio Hondo county fair—"

"I know, that's why we moved down here."

"Not even you could take that bank, boss," warned Belle. "It's got one of the latest, strongest safes I've ever seen."

"You'd know about those kind of things, of course," Anna purred.

"A feller I knew real good told me, and *he* knew. But you could make a good haul with less trouble, boss."

"Where?"

"At the OD Connected ranch house."

Anna let out a bellowing snort of laughter. "You're *loco*, Winnie."

"No, boss," answered Belle, accepting the use of her assumed name. "It'll be easy. Ole Devil always keeps plenty of cash on hand, he buys cattle from down in Mexico. The money's in his safe. I've heard Mark Counter say there's usually around ten thousand dollars in the safe."

"And a full ranch crew on hand to guard it," Anna pointed out.

"Not while the county fair's on, boss. Last year there weren't but three men on the place, the rest being in town for the fun."

"And Ole Devil keeps his money out there?"

"He allowed that nobody'd dare to steal it because of his floating outfit."

"Only, Mark Counter and Dusty Fog are dead," Belle Starr put in.

At the mention of Mark's name for a second time, Calamity stirred uneasily on the bed. Then her eyes focused on the blond's face. To her amazement, Calamity saw Belle's eye close in a wink. Suddenly, without needing words, Calamity knew the truth. Mark Counter was alive, the reports of his death faked to lull the Bad Bunch's suspicions. Only with an effort of will did Calamity hold down her whoop of delight and remain as motionless as ever.

"Taking the safe'd be as easy as stealing pie," Belle Boyd went on.

"You know a lot for a maid," Ina purred, toying as usual with the hilt of her knife.

"This feller I knew told me. He planned to take it himself, but got drunk and mean in Polveroso City and Hondo Fog had to kill him."

"Ten thousand dollars," Anna said softly. "What kind of safe is it?"

"An old one, boss. Sam, the feller, allowed he could open it with his boot, although I reckon it'd be a mite harder. Like I said, Ole Devil relied more on the floating outfit to scare folks off."

Sitting back in her chair, Anna read nothing but a desire to please and make good on Belle's face. Anna drummed her big fingers on the tabletop as she turned the information over in her mind. Such a hit would hurt Ole Devil Hardin's finances and pride. It would be a further blow at the man who sent out Company C on the mission that finished her guerrilla band. Not that she cared a damn about the men who died—in fact she sacrificed them so that she might escape—but the defeat rankled. Never would she forgive the men responsible for smashing the band that her driving force created.

"We'll go to the Rio Hondo," she declared.

"Into town, boss?" Mitzi inquired.

"There's a line cabin about half a day's ride from Polveroso," Belle Boyd put in. "It's never used much and less so during the county fair."

"We'll look it over," Anna promised, and glanced at Calamity. "How soon will you be fit to ride, Belle?"

"Right now," Calamity answered, "If your gal can."

"I don't reckon Tawny feels like it," Anna smiled. "Or you, come to that. We'll give it a couple of days. Then we'll arrive toward the end of the fair week and there'll be less chance the line cabin being used."

"Smart thinking," complimented Calamity. "Say, do you reckon this pair can care for my hoss?"

"You rest up, I'll see they do," Anna replied, pleased with praise from the most famous female outlaw of the day.

"Have them tote my gear in here," Calamity suggested. "They used my name and I reckon they should pay for it."

"They're yours, Belle," smiled Anna. "You hear me, you pair?"

"Yes, boss," chorused the two Belles.

Among the other items in her bedroll, Calamity had brought along a small parfleche bag of homemade medicines. A whiskey bottle contained an oil made up by an Indian medicine woman and Calamity stripped off her clothes, then ordered Belle Starr to apply the lotion carefully to her sore frame. How effective it proved to be showed when Calamity rose the next morning in reasonably good shape, while Tawny could barely move for the stiffness in her limbs. Always a good-hearted girl, Calamity wanted to offer Tawny a share of the soothing oil, but the two Belles were against the idea. Nothing Calamity could do would lessen the defeated girl's hate, and the longer she remained incapacitated the better for all concerned.

During the next two days no chance presented itself to jump the Bad Bunch. While trusting Calamity to a certain extent, Anna watched her and did not offer to return either the Navy Colt nor the Winchester carbine from the buckskin's saddle. Neither of the Belles had a chance to retrieve their arms, taken from them by their guides when approaching the hideout. Despite all Anna's efforts the trio managed to get together in private, and Belle Boyd told of the arrangements made with Betty Hardin. After hearing them, Belle Starr and Calamity agreed to wait.

At last the party left their camp. Traveling mostly by night, as the girls had when drawing close to the rendezvous, avoiding contact with other human beings, they followed the Ronde River to its junction with the Rio Hondo. Give Anna Gould her due, she not only possessed good army maps, but knew how to use them. Once on the OD Connected range Belle guided them to the line cabin and, after scouting it carefully, Anna pronounced it satisfactory for their needs.

"It's Thursday today," she said on the evening of their arrival. "We'll lay up here until Saturday and then Ina, Tawny, Belle, and Winnie'll go with me to the ranch house."

"There's been nobody up this way for a few days," Calamity remarked. "I'm getting sick of hardtack and beans. So tomorrow I'll take Winnie and Sadie out to see if I can get us some deer meat."

"Sadie and Dora," corrected Anna. "I need Winnie here to make sure I know everything about the house."

"You're the boss," Calamity said amiably, despite her disappointment at not managing to have her friends with her. "I'll take my carbine and Colt, though."

"Sure, Belle," Anna agreed, and Tawny let out a disapproving sniff but said nothing.

On waking late the following morning, the remainder of the party found Tawny had already left the cabin. Mitzi offered an explanation, claiming that Tawny said she intended to go hunting and show that redheaded cow how it should be done. Knowing that Tawny always handled the outfit's hunting, and was still smarting under her defeat at "Belle Starr's" hands, Anna saw nothing to feel concerned about in the disappearance.

Although she wore her gun belt, with the loaded and capped Colt holstered in it, and carried the carbine, Calamity had not been able to produce a weapon for Belle. Claiming that the blond did not need a gun for her part, Anna refused to return Belle's Manhattan Navy revolver or loan her one of the Bad Bunch's arms. Rather than create suspicion, Calamity did not press the point and cheerfully agreed that, as Dora carried a rifle, they only needed "Sadie" along to do the heavy toting.

The line cabin had been built in the days before Dusty Fog and the Ysabel Kid helped persuade the Comanches to make peace and move onto a reservation.*

* Told in *Sidewinder.*

It sat in a small valley, a refuge hidden from view by sloping, bush-dotted folds of land. On two occasions members of the OD Connected crew hid there undetected while Indian raiding parties went by. Looking back as she rode away, Calamity realized that the place would strike any owlhoot planning such a robbery as an ideal base for the raid.

Apart from Tawny, none of the girls rose early and the time passed noon before Calamity's party took to their horses. Nor did they find quarry for almost two hours. At last, however, Calamity's carbine tumbled over a white-tail buck incautious enough to let her come within fifty yards before deciding to run. While gathering about the body to start butchering it, the girls heard the sound of approaching hooves. Turning, they saw a small, beautiful, black-haired girl dressed in a shirtwaist and denim pants riding towards them on a good-quality roan horse.

"That's Betty Hardin!" Dora hissed. "I've heard Winnie describe her."

Calamity and Belle exchanged glances. One of the things Belle Boyd told them was that she arranged to steer the Bad Bunch to the line cabin, using the county fair and chance to rob Ole Devil's home as bait. Although there had been no sign of it, the floating outfit probably kept the cabin under observation after Belle left San Antone with Mitzi. From what both Belle Starr and Calamity knew of Betty Hardin, they did not doubt that she insisted on taking her full share of the watching. By sheer bad luck, she appeared to be alone and continued to ride in the trio's direction.

Give Betty credit, she did not ride up full of arrogant assumption that nobody dare interfere with Ole Devil's granddaughter. When she saw the girls, her first inclination had been to hide, make sure they hid out at the line cabin, and then head for the ranch house as fast as her horse could run. Not until she recognized Belle Starr and Calamity, from photographs in Mark's possession, did she offer to let herself be seen. While not sure how the two girls came to be involved, Betty knew them to be allies and hoped to learn of Belle Boyd's fate.

Her arrival handed Calamity and Belle one hell of a problem: deciding how they should act. Having heard from the floating outfit of Betty's special talents, Belle decided that the Texan girl might bring the odds down to where a chance of taking the Bad Bunch would be worth taking.

"Let's grab her!" Belle hissed. "I bet the boss'll find some use for her."

"Yeah," agreed Dora. "I reckon Anna'll be real pleased when she sees that we've brought in a prime hostage."

Which comment only went to prove that Dora was a lousy prophetess.

Acting just as if the kidnapping were real, Calamity and Belle covered and searched a suitably behaving Betty. Then they loaded the deer onto Calamity's buckskin and started back to the line cabin by a roundabout route. The sun hung down in the western sky as they rode up to the cabin. To one side stood Tawny's horse, lathered and showing signs of hard use. As usual Anna kept her mount saddled and ready to ride close to the building. Ordering her two companions to off-load the deer, Calamity told Betty to dismount and not try anything. Already the other women emerged from the cabin and approached, with Tawny hanging behind them.

"Where're the boys?" Calamity whispered to Betty.

"They had to go into town to help Uncle Hondo handle some trouble. It looks like we'll have to take them, Calam."

"Who's she?" demanded Anna, ignoring the two girls as they dumped the deer on the ground. "What took you so long?"

"She's Ole Devil's granddaughter, no less," Calamity replied. "And she's what took us so long."

"You mean to say that you brought her here!" Anna shouted.

"She found us just after we dropped the buck," Calamity snapped back. "We should maybe have shot her and left her there to be found?"

"Why not?"

"Because I figured she'd be worth less dead than alive."

"Mitzi, Carrie, grab hold of that gal and haul her up to the cabin," Anna ordered. "Tromp her some if she gives you any fuss."

While Betty might have given considerable fuss, she meekly submitted to having one girl take a double-handed hold of each wrist. However, Mitzi and Carrie did not obey immediately. Sensing a dramatic development, they contented themselves with holding Betty's arms and waited to learn what happened next.

"I reckon Ole Devil'll pay well to get her back," Calamity told Anna. "And she'll make a jim-dandy hostage happen anybody finds us."

"They'll be looking for her," Anna pointed out.

"I can't see what you're worrying about, boss," Belle Boyd put in. "With Dusty Fog and Mark Counter dead, that outfit's nothing."

"Then it's something again," Tawny put in, stepping to one side of the others and lining her Bulldog at Calamity.

"She gone *loco*, Anna?" demanded Calamity.

"What's up, Tawny?" Anna barked. "You've not said two words since you came back here."

"I've been thinking instead of talking!" Tawny hissed, never moving the revolver's barrel out of line. "Thinking about these three here. How it was mighty strange that all of a sudden they'd decide they wanted to join up with us."

"We told you why," Calamity said. "Only you wasn't listening too good that day." Her eyes went to Anna. "The licking I gave her must've shook what passes for brains up, boss."

"I went into Polveroso today," Tawny said, the words dripping out as if each carried a load of poison. "It's a mighty interesting place for seeing ghosts."

Calamity watched the other all the time she spoke and stayed very still. Maybe she could handle a gun better than Tawny, but not to the extent of getting her Colt clear and throwing lead against the other's advantage. Given only a moment of inattention, the redhead figured to make her move; but Tawny watched her all the time.

"How do you mean, ghosts?" asked Anna.

"Either that—or Mark Counter's alive."

"Ali . . ." began the boss of the Bad Bunch, emotions playing on her face.

"That's right!" Tawny screeched. "He's alive. I saw him in Polvero—"

At which point Betty, guessing from the first mention of Polveroso what Tawny must have seen, made her move. The girls holding her stood staring at Tawny but not releasing their grips. Allowing the hold on her arms to maintain her balance, Betty shifted her weight onto the left leg and bent it slightly. Up rose her right foot and shot sideways at Mitzi. Betty wore riding boots and the hard edge of the sole collided with the front of Mitzi's shin, then slid down the thinly covered bone. Even as Mitzi screeched in pain and released her hold, Betty began to pivot toward Carrie. Moving at speed, Betty whipped her freed arm across. Held for the *hiranukite* of karate, Betty's fingers drove straight into Carrie's left breast. A cry of pain broke from the bigger girl and she, too, lost her hold. Before Betty could make a move to help her friends, Mitzi, tears pouring down plump cheeks and face twisted in mingled pain and fury, stopped clutching the kicked shin, plunged forward to tackle the little Texan around the waist and brought her down.

Hearing Mitzi, Tawny could not prevent herself from glancing around and in doing so her Bulldog wavered slightly. Calamity needed no more. It was not a chance one wanted to take but the redhead figured she had nothing to lose under the circumstances. As Tawny held the gun in her right hand, Calamity dived to the left and grabbed for the Colt as she went.

At the redhead's first move, Tawny jerked her eyes away from Betty's captors and squeezed the Bulldog's trigger. Calamity felt as if somebody had pressed a hot iron against her side, knew she had been nicked by the bullet but did not panic. Out came the Colt in a move well practiced but never before used against another human being. For all that Calamity did not hesitate. On landing upon the grass, she pressed the Colt's trigger and released the hammer. Powder smoke momentarily blurred Calamity's vision, yet she saw enough through it. Tawny jerked, a hole appearing in her chest just over the V of the shirt's neck. Shocked pain twisted her face, her hand fell to her side, and the Bulldog dropped from limp fingers. She followed it to the ground.

"Get them!" Anna screamed.

Letting out a low hiss of suppressed excitement, Ina flicked out her knife. Much as Belle Starr wanted to deal with the girl who knifed Mark Counter, she had no chance to do so. Being the closest of the law's side to Anna, Belle knew she must be the one to tackle the big woman, a task she did not relish but tried to begin. Even as Belle started toward the big woman and saw the Remington Double Derringer slide from its sleeve holster, Dora attacked her from the side. Two arms locked around Belle's waist and the weight of Dora's body bore her to the ground. After which Dora rapidly wished that she had not made the move. On their first meeting,

Belle fought Calamity Jane until they both collapsed exhausted and had lost none of her skill. Not that Belle had things all her own way, Dora being a tough girl in her own right and well versed in such matters.

"Ina!" Belle Boyd shouted as the blond started toward where Calamity, left hand pressed to her bleeding side, tried to rise.

Hearing Belle's voice, Ina swung around. One quick look warned Belle of the danger she faced. Ina came in with deadly precision, body crouching slightly on flexed knees so as to give her security and extreme mobility. Close to her body, handle held diagonally across the palm of her right hand, the knife slanted toward Belle. At the same time Ina kept her left hand extended for balance and to distract the other girl with sudden movements, grabs, and gestures. That stance offered the best protection against an attacker armed also with a knife served as a guard should the other try to use a club or chair and put an unarmed opponent in an exceedingly dangerous position.

If possible, the expression on Ina's face made things far worse. The wild, almost ecstatic play of emotions on the angelic face, eyes glinting with anticipation, made Belle realize what she had suspected all the time: Ina was mentally deranged and found pleasure in killing. Facing an efficient armed girl would be bad enough, but a madwoman with such ability . . .

The knife made a flickering arc toward Belle's stomach. Forcing her fears down, she danced aside and kicked, her foot driving into the blond's thigh. For the first time Ina received physical pain; the other members of the Bad Bunch never dared pick a quarrel with her. A screech almost animal in its tone burst from her and she brought back the knife. Once more Belle moved, yet almost too late, so fast did the blond strike. Cloth ripped as the knife's clipped point cut through Belle's shirt and made a shallow gash across her torso just under the bust. Belle felt a stinging sensation, knew that she had been nicked if nothing worse, caught her balance, and made a high kick, which caught Ina under the jaw. If that kick had landed with full strength, it might have broken the blond's jaw and certainly would put her down. At extreme range, the kick only arrived hard enough to hurt. It made Ina reel back without causing her to drop the knife.

Once more Ina screamed and her face distorted in hideous rage. Forgetting caution, though not losing her deadly stance, she attacked again. Belle leaped aside and the force of Ina's rush carried her by. Snapping a kick to the back of Ina's knee, Belle destroyed her balance. Like a flash Belle kicked again, her foot driving into Ina's back with all the force she could manage. Ina screamed and shot forward, her impetus and the second kick hurling her toward where the white-tail buck lay on the ground. Its neck had twisted when the girls laid it down and jaw rested upon the grass while its hatrack head of horns stood erect. Too late Ina saw her danger, if she recognized it in her state of crazed fury. Completely off balance, she fell forward onto the buck's compact, powerful antlers. A scream broke from her as the rising tines bit into her flesh.

During her life Belle Boyd had seen gruesome sights, but none so hideous as the small, beautiful girl draped, impaled through stomach and breast, on the antlers of the dead buck. Forgetting her own injury, Belle ran forward to try to save Ina. One glance told Belle that she came too late.

Anna Gould stood for once in the throes of indecision, unable to select the most dangerous of her enemies. Already Tawny lay dead or dying and, even as Anna watched, Ina plunged to her fate.

"Turn 'round, Anna!" Calamity yelled, ignoring the pain in her side and kneeling up, ready to shoot.

At the sound Anna reached her decision. Realizing

that she had been tricked, she saw with terrible clarity the full danger of her position. Most likely men were already coming and she guessed that they would have little respect for her sex, knowing her to be the boss of the Bad Bunch. So she must escape. Of all her band only Tawny and Ina meant anything to her, and they because of the talents she trained into them. Neither were of any further use and the other three did not count.

The reign of the Bad Bunch had come to an end. No longer would they have a cloak of anonymity to shield them in their activities. Once word got around, and every peace officer had been given her description, entering even a town crowded with strangers could only be done with the greatest risk. That did not matter greatly. The loot from their various jobs, even after deductions for the rest of the gang, had been stashed away safely and ought to keep her in comfort back east for the rest of her life. So she deserted the remainder of her gang, relying on them to hold the attention of the young women who tricked her.

Bringing up her Colt, Calamity squeezed off a shot and missed. She tried to rise fast, gasped in pain, and sank down again. Before she could regain control of herself, she saw Anna disappear around the side of the cabin and remembered the waiting horse. Unless something could be done, Anna Gould might yet escape. Gritting her teeth, Calamity dragged herself erect and started toward the cabin.

As she came into sight of her horse, Anna saw a shape appear in the cranberry bushes some twenty yards away. A small man in cowhand's clothes, but to Anna he seemed to tower like an avenging giant.

"You!" she screamed, skidding to a halt and firing the derringer.

On reaching Polveroso City, Dusty learned that his father had the trouble—a quartet of young outlaws holed up in a small cabin after rashly attempting to rob a saloon—well in hand. There being work to do at the ranch, he left his two friends to enjoy the final day of the county fair and returned to the OD Connected. Hearing that Betty rode out, Dusty guessed at her destination. He waited only long enough to throw a saddle on a fresh mount before starting after the girl. Although Dusty did not claim to be in the Kid's class as a reader of tracks, he saw enough to tell him of Betty's "abduction." From the lack of sign, Dusty concluded that his cousin went quietly with her captors. That hinted she knew at least one of the female trio. Saying a number of uncomplimentary things about Betty's impulsive nature, Dusty headed for the line cabin. On arrival, he left his horse some distance back and moved in on foot. Hearing the start of the fighting, he dashed forward and came into sight of the saddled horse by the cabin. Even as he remembered "Hannah's" habit of keeping a horse saddled ready for escape, the woman appeared.

Dusty missed death by inches as the derringer's bullet cut the air by his head. Instantly and instinctively his hands crossed, flickering almost faster than the eye could follow as they reached for, gripped, and drew the white-handled Colts. Three-quarters of a second did not give Dusty time to think of Anna's sex or allow considerations of her being a woman to slow his hand. He knew she meant to kill him if she could, and had brought death to many people during her career of crime, yet he might even then have hesitated, given time to think. Instead he drew and fired in a bare three-quarters of a second, ripping two .44 bullets into Anna's head as she cocked the derringer for a second shot.

With shocking impact Dusty realized that he had shot a woman. Before the feeling could take fully hold, he again heard the sounds of the fighting in front of the cabin and knew he must make some move. In passing, he glanced down at the body sprawled on the ground. One bullet had torn through her left eye, the other made its hole just over the right, while the ground beneath the body turned red as blood gashed from the shattered base of the skull.

Feeling ready to fetch up, Dusty went by the body. At first he meant to go help Betty as she held Mitzi's neck trapped between her legs and applied a stranglehold that rapidly ended Carrie's inclination to fight. Seeing Calamity's wound, Dusty went toward her, but the redhead waved him by.

"I-I'll do, Dusty," she gritted. "Go help Belle Boyd."

Belle Starr might not be getting things all her own way, but she clearly needed no help. So Dusty went to where Belle Boyd stood by Ina and tried to draw the shrieking blond from the antlers. Although the sight made Dusty feel sick in his stomach, he eased Belle aside and drew the injured girl from the impaling tines. As he lay Ina on the ground, she went limp and unconscious. Dusty knew that only a trained doctor acting immediately might hope to save the girl's life. As the nearest doctor was in Polveroso, Ina's only hope would be that she died without regaining consciousness.

Then he saw the blood on the front of Belle's clothes. "She cut you!" he said.

"N-Not badly," Belle replied, and fainted.

At that moment Belle Starr landed a punch that stretched Dora out and ended their fight. Bruised, bloody, with her shirt torn open, Belle rose and stared around. Releasing a limp, unresisting Carrie's neck, Betty sat up and heaved Mitzi away from her. More than half-strangled, the plump girl landed on her side, rolled onto her face, and lay sobbing in exhaustion. Slowly Betty rose, swaying on her feet. Then she staggered over to where Dusty knelt at Belle Boyd's side.

"Is she . . . ?"

"Got a bad nick and fainted, is all," Dusty answered. "The other gal's dead."

"The big woman's escaped, Dusty!" Betty gasped,

looking around to where Belle Starr raised Calamity from the ground.

"I got her, Betty," Dusty replied in a strangled voice. "The Bad Bunch's done for good."

16

AS BAD AS
A WOMAN COULD GET

For once women outnumbered the men in Ole Devil's gun-decorated study. Claiming that her injury—Tawny's bullet broke a rib as it glanced off—gave her the right to extra comfort, Calamity annexed Mark Counter's pet chair by the fireplace. Belle Starr curled in the Kid's seat opposite, while Betty Hardin perched on the arm of Dusty's chair. Despite her stitched and bandaged wound, Belle Boyd stood facing the others. Dusty's mother had come out from Polveroso on hearing of the fight and stood at the table setting out coffee and sandwiches, her presence giving the females a voting majority over Ole Devil and the three members of his floating outfit.

It was Sunday evening and they gathered to talk over the events that had caused each girl to sustain injury.

"I learned a fair bit from Mitzi on the ride from San Antone and the other two filled in some of the missing details when I saw them in town this afternoon," Belle said. "You remember 'Hannah's' guerrillas, Dusty?"

"Sure. Tawny and the big woman were with them

when Company C wiped them out at the end of the war."

"The big woman's name was Anna Gould," Belle remarked, feeling entitled to a little grand drama after what she had been through.

"So?" asked Dusty, then his face changed expression. "Anna . . . You can't mean that . . ."

"I can," Belle assured him. "She was 'Hannah.' What everybody assumed to be the surname of the male leader was really her Christian name. I learned some of the story from Mitzi, who got it from Tawny and some of the older women. When Company C found the guerrilla camp, Anna counted on you still not thinking a woman could be their leader. She came out to see what chance they had in a fight and decided there was none. So she pretended to accept your offer of safe passage for the girls and went back. In the cabin she told the men that she aimed to take the girls out, and go up and destroy the cannon while they distracted your troops' attention. Maybe the men wouldn't have believed her, but they saw it was their only hope. Pretending to be fetching a Ketchum grenade to use on the gun, she went into the store cellar. Only instead of collecting the grenade, she left a burning fuse running into one of the gunpowder kegs."

"And when it went off, we figured that Hannah died inside," Dusty said.

"Yes. Anna had enough of a hold on the women for them not to betray her, but she thought some of the men might when you took the remaining cabins. So she slipped away, collected a horse she kept hidden away from the cabins, and escaped."

"All the men died fighting and the women kept quiet," Dusty remarked.

"You left them in the hands of the Yankees," Belle went on. "With the end of the war, they turned Tawny and the others free rather than waste time on them.

Anna found the girl and started planning their life of crime."

"How about the other girl, Ina?" asked Betty.

"She was Tracey Prince's blond with a face like an angel," Dusty told her.

"That's right," Belle agreed. "Mitzi told me about her, too. It seems that Ina was raised in a Quaker village that Anna's band planned to raid. Only one of the gang took the girl away on the night before the raid. What he didn't know was that Ina hated anybody to hold her. She killed him the night they left the village, in one of the band's hideouts. Anna found her there and took her along when she went after Tawny. I don't know much about the next couple of years, but Mitzi thinks they went to either Chicago or New York. Wherever it was, Anna learned how to break safes, and taught the two girls their parts. At last she came back West, with a pair of killers as deadly as any Texas gunfighter. She built up an organization, selecting saloon girls and using the women from her old guerrilla band to gather information. She picked them well, for they stayed loyal to her."

"Not all of them," Calamity intervened. "That's how I got onto them. One of her girls couldn't stand the killing they did and ran out. She told a saloon gal I'd done a big favor for and the gal passed the word to me after we heard about Mark being killed." Her eyes went to the blond giant. "Let me know next time you *don't* get killed, you big ox."

"I'll do just that," promised Mark, avoiding Belle Starr's accusing eyes.

"So young Prince found his gal at last," Ole Devil said quietly.

"Yes, sir," Belle Boyd replied. "Apparently she always wore a disguise in town, until acting as lookout or fire raiser on the job. We found a wig and rubber cheek pads among her belongings. It seems that despite the disguise Tracey Prince recognized her—by her voice, maybe. Instead of following McKie, he went to her hotel. Anna saw him and decided he must die. So Ina removed her disguise, slipped out of her room, lured him down to the corral, and killed him."

"Poor Tracey," Betty sighed. "After all that time searching, when he found his girl, she killed him. Lord! What made her that way?"

"Likely we'll never know," Dusty answered. "How about the hit at the Fort Worth county offices? Why'd they change their way of working?"

"Anna decided they could do it better in daylight. She planned to hit all the banks and the Wells Fargo office, too, but learned of their guards," Belle Boyd explained. "The town was all but deserted and they might have succeeded. She sent Ina to the barn to keep watch, but to start a fire only if people came back to town or if it seemed likely that the other two would be discovered."

"I reckon folks can rest easier in their beds now the Bad Bunch's done," Ole Devil commented. "How many folks died because they saw women and didn't realize the danger?"

"Too many, sir," Belle Boyd replied. "Anna Gould was as bad as a woman could get."

"I'd never killed a woman," Dusty put in quietly.

"Don't regret doing it, Dusty," Belle told him. "If ever one deserved to die, it was Anna Gould."

Thinking of the number of people killed by the Bad Bunch at her instigation, Dusty felt inclined to agree. Yet he still wished there had been some other way of dealing with her. At the back of his thoughts, he knew there had not been and that Anna Gould had met a well-deserved end.

John Jakes

Hailed by the *Los Angeles Times* as "the godfather of historical novels," John Jakes' masterfully researched Civil War trilogy follows the lives and times of the Mains of South Carolina and the Hazards of Pennsylvania, two American families torn by the fiery politics that divided North and South.

☐ **HEAVEN AND HELL**   20170-5 $5.95

☐ **LOVE AND WAR**   15016-7 $5.95

The epic TV mini-series…

☐ **NORTH AND SOUTH**
(A Dell/HBJ Book)   16205-X $5.95